ODDBODY

STORIES

ROSE KEATING

Simon & Schuster Paperbacks

NEW YORK AMSTERDAM/ANTWERP LONDON
TORONTO SYDNEY/MELBOURNE NEW DELHI

Simon & Schuster Paperbacks
An Imprint of Simon & Schuster, LLC
1230 Avenue of the Americas
New York, NY 10020

This book is a work of fiction. Any references to historical events, real people, or real places are used fictitiously. Other names, characters, places, and events are products of the author's imagination, and any resemblance to actual events or places or persons, living or dead, is entirely coincidental.

First Simon & Schuster trade paperback edition July 2025

SIMON & SCHUSTER PAPERBACKS and colophon are registered trademarks of Simon & Schuster, LLC

Simon & Schuster strongly believes in freedom of expression and stands against censorship in all its forms. For more information, visit BooksBelong.com.

For information about special discounts for bulk purchases, please contact Simon & Schuster Special Sales at 1-866-506-1949 or business@simonandschuster.com.

The Simon & Schuster Speakers Bureau can bring authors to your live event. For more information or to book an event, contact the Simon & Schuster Speakers Bureau at 1-866-248-3049 or visit our website at www.simonspeakers.com.

Interior design by Paul Dippolito

Manufactured in the United States of America

1   3   5   7   9   10   8   6   4   2

Library of Congress Cataloging-in-Publication Data is available on file.

ISBN 978-1-6680-6150-3
ISBN 978-1-6680-6151-0 (ebook)

CONTENTS

ODDBODY

ODDBODY

You like the ghost a lot. You think it's good company. It's chatty and charming, and it often makes you laugh. The ghost has excellent taste in French absurdist cinema and enjoys listening to ska from time to time. The ghost is a good listener. The ghost doesn't mind that you like to gossip. The ghost has a real knack for crossword puzzles. You do wish the ghost would stop encouraging you to kill yourself, but you know that it's intended in a nice way.

'It's not that I want you to die,' the ghost says, floating its Monopoly piece four places, 'I just think it's important for you to try new things.'

You pick up the dice. They are firm and solid in your hand. You don't want to let them go. 'I like living,' you say, dropping the dice onto the board.

'Why?'

'It feels good.'

'What about it feels good?'

'I don't know. Sunshine. Chocolate. Sex. They're good. Having a body feels good.'

'I don't know,' the ghost says. The ghost solidifies, the gaseous silver of its form gathering itself into droplets that hang in a glister in the air. It's a cloud of rain shaped like a person. It frowns at you. 'Sounds overrated.'

'Don't you remember?'

'Do you remember being born?'

'No.'

The ghost picks up the dice. 'It's very ugly and painful.' Its hand is dripping all over the board. You'll have to buy a new one, again. The ghost shakes its head. 'You wouldn't want to remember,' it says.

※

Ben pours the wine too quickly, splashing his palm and wrist. He lifts his wrist to your mouth. You laugh because you think he is joking. When he doesn't move his wrist, you poke your tongue out just a little and glance up to check if this is correct. He smiles in approval. You swipe your tongue across his heart line—the skin is thin here, and you can feel the beat of his slow, heavy pulse.

'Nice?' he asks. You nod.

'Yuck,' the ghost says.

Ben whips his wrist back, looking around the kitchen. The ghost isn't visible. It usually isn't when he visits. 'Can you make it go away?' he asks.

'There's not much I can really do,' you say.

'It makes me uncomfortable. I think it hates me.'

'Of course it doesn't hate you.'

'Yes, I do,' a voice says from somewhere above. You frown at the ceiling and try to subtly shake your head at it.

The ghost is silent for the rest of the evening. Ben told you he would cook for you. He has brought a bag of ingredients that are incomprehensible in tandem: ham, dried currants, bamboo shoots, bicarbonate of soda, powdered custard, truffle oil, saffron, a single large and softened onion. You watch him cut the onion; it is satisfying to see his long, delicate fingers press the knife through the pulpy heart.

He puts the knife down and kisses you instead. He leads you to the bedroom, and then leads you to the bed. You lean backwards, flicking off the light when he slips off your underwear. He leaves the skirt on, his face hidden under it while he eats you out, his thin mouth rough. You think about how you can't see his expression and when you come the feeling hits you as hard as grief. He stands after you finish.

'That was fun,' he says. He kisses your forehead. You reach for his crotch and he steps away.

'I'm a little tired,' he says.

'Oh,' you say. Your hands stutter in the air, unsure where they are meant to be. He goes to leave, opening the door. He stops for a second and turns back to you.

'Doireann, I think you should get help. With the ghost. It's a bit much,' he says. He walks out and closes the door before you can reply.

You sit on the bed and stare at the door. Eventually, you figure out how to move your hands again and turn on the lamp. You pluck a tissue out of the box on your nightstand and spread your legs. The cold air is cruel as you wipe between your thighs. The tissue comes away viscous and sodden, slimed over with a thick, gelatinous substance.

'Sickening,' the ghost says. The particles of its form surround you, gathering you in grey mist.

'I know.'

'Why would you do that?'

'I can't help it. It's just what it does.'

'You could help it. Stop having sex with him.'

'It feels nice. He's nice.'

The ghost sucks the tissue from your hand, floating it over your face. This close, you can smell yourself, musty and sour, faintly metallic. The substance has begun to congeal in the cool air.

'So nice,' the ghost says.

You wash your hands in the kitchen sink, scrubbing between your fingers with grapefruit dish soap. You look at the onion on the wooden board, smell the pungent stink of its half-chopped heart. The other ingredients are gone; you are unsure if he took them back home, or if he tidied them away. You decide not to check.

You pick up the board and bring it out to the front garden, scraping the sloppy layers out into the compost bin. The ghost watches you from the doorstep, shaking its head. It turns around, walks back inside. You linger in the garden, chopping board in hand. The cold stings your feet, but you don't really mind.

'There're practicalities, though. You never think about the practicalities,' you say, walking past the cereal aisle towards the tins at the back of the shop. The ghost follows beside you; you can't see it, but you can feel it, the heaviness in the atmosphere. Occasionally, it tickles your palm and pulls at the ends of your hair.

'Like what?' it asks.

'It would hurt. Wouldn't it hurt?'

'I don't know. Lots of things hurt when you're alive. It wouldn't hurt after.'

You pick up a can of tinned spaghetti. The tin is snatched from your hand. It flies back onto the shelf.

'The sauce will upset your stomach. Everything upsets your stomach. You should go to a doctor. There's probably something wrong with you,' the ghost says. 'Cancer, maybe.'

On the other side of the aisle, you see a young man with his eyes shut tight. His face is pale and covered in a layer of sweat. A ghost stands next to him, holding on to his hand. It's whispering something in his ear. The man nods and then lets out a low whimper. Water leaks out from the ghost's mouth and drips down the man's trousers, puddling on the floor at their feet. The security guard frowns at them. He catches your eye and grimaces, then grins. You grimace back; it is lovely to be a person included in a private joke or look.

You pick the tin back up and hold it as tight as you can. 'Cop on,' you whisper to your ghost, hoping the guard is too far to hear.

You go to the till, unloading your shopping. The ghost pretends to help. It levitates the broccoli, followed by the milk and rice, whizzing them around in circles above your head before lowering them back onto the belt. You try to save the eggs, but the ghost sucks each one out of the packet, twirling them in 360 spins so fast that they let out a high-pitched whistle.

The shopkeeper raises her head, looking up at the spinning eggs. She lowers her gaze to you, brows furrowed. 'Are you all right?' she asks.

'Yeah?' You pass her the groceries and she scans them through. Her movements are slow and cautious, as if you might drop the items. She glances between the ghost and you while you pack the shopping. The lines of her mouth crinkle when she frowns.

You hand her the money. She takes it, but her hand lingers. Her fingers brush yours.

'You'd want to watch yourself, love,' she says quietly.

The eggs above your head stop spinning, and then they shatter. The innards fall on your face and on the shopkeeper's hands. The money glistens, gold with yolk.

'Oops,' the ghost says.

'I'm so sorry,' you say. You grab the empty carton of eggs and stuff it into the shopping bag and leave. Egg drips from your face. Your hair is drenched in it; it's heavy as mucus and splatters when it falls to the floor.

When you get home, the ghost is apologetic. It doesn't say much, but it makes sad, keening noises. It places blankets around your shoulders, heats up the hot water bottle, floats you cup after cup after cup of milky tea. When you shower, it plucks eggshells out of the roots of your hair, gently untwisting the knots where they hide.

You spend hours of your evenings drafting messages to Ben. You write rough first drafts on paper scraps in biro, then transfer them to a Word document to edit. After editing, you type them into the Notes app on your phone. You retype them again in Ben's message box, scanning the words for energy, humour, lightness of tone. You delete them before you can press send.

One time you do send him a video of a puppy playing with a turtle. You send another text apologising and say you meant to send it to someone else. He opens the messages and does not reply.

You met Ben for the first time through a dating app, and you thought that meant he wanted to date you. He asked you to go for coffee. You planned to wear minimal makeup and cozy wool, planned to look loveable. You realised this was not possible. You wore the dress that sometimes exposed your nipples, wore the lipstick that cracked if you smiled with teeth.

You smiled with your mouth closed when you spotted Ben inside the café. He was seated by the window, his light hair catching sunbeams. He stood when he spotted you.

'Wow,' Ben said. He smiled. 'I mean, wow.'

You laughed. You opened your mouth to say something, and the ghost spewed out of your throat in a wet gush, splashing all over the floor. It looked up at Ben. 'She wants you inside her,' it said.

Ben's mouth twisted, upper lip curling. He seemed disgusted, and then he seemed intrigued. He scanned you over and suggested that you both go back to your place.

He didn't ask you to go for coffee again after that.

❧

You and the ghost sunbathe together in the garden. You sprawl on separate sun loungers; the ghost doesn't really need one, but you think it appreciates the gesture.

The ghost is beautiful today. It is more solid than it's been in weeks; it has a torso and a head and things that almost look like fingers and toes. The droplets of its body catch the light and refract it; every time it moves, it throws out a rainbow.

'There're ways to do it that wouldn't hurt, probably,' it says.

You turn the page of your book. 'I don't want to talk about this today.'

'You're thinking about this all wrong. It doesn't have to be a bad thing.'

You hum. You bring the book to your nose and breathe in. Vanilla, coffee, dust. You heard somewhere that old books smell that way because of chemical rot. You think it smells sweet either way.

'If I did it, I wouldn't be able to finish this book. I would like to finish this book.'

'That's a bit presumptuous. Maybe you still could. You don't know.'

'Can you read, after? Is there a heaven?'

'Can't tell you.'

'Why not?'

It taps the side of its nose. 'Ghost code.'

'If there was a heaven, why wouldn't you stay there?'

'Because I like you, and I want to help you.'

You pick up a strawberry from the side table and pop it in your mouth. It's tart and ripe and so tender that it falls apart before it reaches your teeth. You stretch your back, letting each bone of your spine crack. The warmth of the sun sinks into your body. You can feel the light settling inside your chest.

'You don't know how good it feels to be alive,' you say. 'Sometimes it just feels so, so good.'

'Only sometimes. It'll hurt again.'

You eat another strawberry. You turn your face to the sun.

'Something awful must have happened to you,' you say.

'Something awful happens to everyone,' the ghost says.

You put on your sunglasses. You continue reading your book.

❦

The ghost likes the call centre.

'I think it's nice. It's mostly just sitting, isn't it? Sitting and listening. It's a lot like being dead, I think. Peaceful,' it says, whispering into your ear. The ghost hides when you are at work. You can feel it hovering over you, but it makes sure to keep out of sight.

You try to tell yourself that you hate the call centre. You should. It's degrading. For eight hours a day strangers tell you over and over that you're a cunt. You apologise for this. You ask them if there is anything else you can do to assist them.

You know you should hate it. But you like it. The repetition puts you in a trance. The words glide over your brain like small bumps on a long train journey, their vibrations lulling you further to sleep. You are somewhere very far away from your body. You wonder if this is how others feel when they meditate.

Across from you, a new girl in glasses is trying to hide the fact that she is crying. You fail to remember her name. She is asking the customer on the phone to explain their problem again, but her voice catches in warped hiccups between words. Her ghost sings loudly and does cartwheels around her desk. Your supervisor Adam watches them, his body very still.

Adam walks over to the girl. He takes the phone from her. He speaks to the customer briefly and hangs up the phone. The room goes quiet when he looks down at the girl, agents pausing calls throughout the office. The ghost continues to sing, the pitch growing higher and higher in the silence.

'Can you explain yourself?' Adam asks.

'I'm so sorry, it's not usually like this,' she says. She rubs her eyes so roughly that you worry the lids will tear.

Adam looks at the ghost, and then at the girl. 'I want you to get your things, and I want you to leave,' he says.

The girl stops rubbing her eyes. 'What?'

'This is a place of business. If you can't act like a professional, you shouldn't be here.'

Her ghost sings in a register so high-pitched that agents cover their ears with their hands. You keep yours firmly by your sides.

'But I'm not the only one with a ghost.'

'You're the only one letting it act out. That's your choice,' he says. He slaps the air next to him. His hand hits an invisible wall; the spot he hits ripples like a puddle. He purses his lips and grabs at the spot, pulling at it with his nails until the head of a ghost emerges, the roots of its hair caught in Adam's fist.

The head is shaking back and forth. It looks frightened.

'You are an adult with agency. You have choices,' Adam says, and swings his other fist at the head.

You expect the fist to glide through the ghost. When the fist connects, you recoil at the splatting, slobbery sound it makes. Like a corpse hitting a lake from a great and brutal height. The force of it splits the ghost's lip, raindrops dribbling from the tear.

The girl's ghost has stopped singing. Its hands cover its mouth.

Adam hits his ghost again, and again, and again. The ghost closes its eyes, taking each hit with a sharp exhale of breath. Sometimes a small whine escapes and it tries to close its mouth. One of its eyes is swollen from the assault. Which is impossible, you think. Because ghosts don't feel pain.

'How are you doing that?' you say.

Adam looks up at you. His own eyes are red and watery, but he smiles warmly. 'I'm a professional,' he says.

After the new girl leaves the office, you feel your ghost between your knees under the desk. Your legs shake. 'Please be good,' you whisper down to it as quietly as you can. The ghost stays quiet for the rest of your shift.

When you open the door to your car, the ghost leans over and places kisses all over your face. They feel like foamy bubbles. It blows raspberries against your cheek until you laugh. On the ride home, it tells you knock-knock jokes. It plays with the radio dials. It mists smiley faces onto the window and elaborately detailed portraits of the band members of Madness. *It's a nice ghost, really*, you think. *The nicest ghost in the world. It's trying its best to be good.*

✸

Sometimes the ghost goes away.

You don't know where. It doesn't happen often. Every now and again you wake in the early hours of the morning, and it is a shock to discover that the air is not heavy with moisture. It is light, buoyant; you wonder if you'll float away on it. You find, for the first time in so long, that it is not a struggle to breathe. That your lungs don't feel sodden. That breathing is natural and easy and wonderful after all.

You place your hands over your eyes. You blink into the dark of your palm. You feel the heat, the gentle tickle of your heartbeat. You are not dead. You are not dead.

The ghost usually comes back while you sleep, but one night you are awake when it returns. It appears at your window, looking in. Behind it are several other ghosts, spinning, dancing, weaving around each other in loops and twirls. Your ghost turns around to say something to them. They look in the window at you and point and grin. It looks like they are laughing at you. Your ghost makes a hushing motion and waves goodbye.

Your ghost floats through the window and over to you, sitting down on the pillow beside you in the dark.

'Hi,' it says.

'Where were you?'

'Out.'

The air is dense again, becoming moist and humid. 'Are you bored of me?' you ask.

The ghost doesn't say anything.

You think, for a moment, about walking away from the ghost. Walking out into the cold, clean night air that would cut through the thickness in your lungs like bleach through scum.

But you *missed* this feeling. You missed this weight between your ribs. The tightness of it feels so very much like being held.

'Please don't leave me,' you say.

You lean into the ghost, pressing your face into the mist of its torso until you are inside of it, immersed in its droplets. The ghost doesn't say anything, but it doesn't leave you either.

❧

Ben invites you over to his apartment.

He's never done this before. When you receive the text, you find yourself smiling at your phone. You reread the text every half hour. You smile every half hour.

Ben is a good host. He takes your coat, makes drinks, plays jazz on a low level from a speaker. He sits you down on the couch and asks you about your day and doesn't acknowledge that you are both just here to have sex. It is very polite of him. You wonder how you got so lucky.

You try to listen to him speak, but you want to snoop. The walls of the apartment are cream, and the floor is a pale wood. There are no photos, no ornaments, no clutter. The couch is white leather, spotless, cool under your fingertips.

He stops talking and leans in to kiss your neck. You spot a novel sticking out of the fold of the couch behind him. 'Hermann Hesse? Is he good?' you say.

He hums. He keeps kissing your neck. You don't stop him. When he leads you to the bedroom, you follow him.

When you reach the bed, you reach out to turn off the lamp on the bedside table. But there is no lamp there, because this isn't your bedroom. He peels your tights from your legs, tossing them aside. He lifts your foot and kisses it, looking up at you as he does so.

'Will we turn off the light?' you say.

He hums again, and moves up your leg, pulling your skirt from you. The air has begun to feel dense, thick; it is like someone pouring concrete down your throat. He unbuttons your blouse.

'The light,' you say.

'Relax,' he says. He reaches behind to undo the clasp of your bra. You close your eyes. You hold your breath.

You feel a drop of something wet fall onto your forehead, and then you hear something shatter.

Ben swears, jumping off you. He stands up, looking at the ceiling. Mist swirls above, surrounding a shattered light bulb. He looks at you, his face shadowed in the semi-dark. His eyes catch the glow of the streetlights beyond the window.

'Did you bring your ghost to my flat?'

Your bra is undone, your breasts hanging limp as dead animals. 'I didn't mean to,' you say.

'Do you not understand how inappropriate this is?'

'It wasn't on purpose, it just came.'

'So? Make it stay at home. Do you not have any control? How can you just let it out in public?'

'I'm trying, I'm sorry, I'm really trying.'

Ben is silent. You wish you could see his face, but it's in shadow. You hear the sound of dripping; the mist still hangs above, leaking droplets onto the wood.

'There are places you can go. For help,' he says. 'There are doctors. Exorcists. There are people who can help. With this kind of thing.'

You hold on to your bra, pressing it against your chest. You try to keep yourself from spilling out.

'It's not that bad, really. It's not a bad ghost. I'm fine, really,' you say.

He stands very still in front of you. 'I think you should probably leave,' he says.

He reaches down and picks up your tights, passing them to you. You grip them in one hand, pull on the blouse with the other. He hands you your shoes, and you hold them close to your chest, clutching them as though they mattered.

As you walk out, you keep your eyes lowered to the ground, on the pristine carpet, your bare feet. You try not to look at the mist lingering on the ceiling, buzzing around the light bulb like a broken hive.

✖

When you open your front door, water comes spilling out, running down over the concrete path that leads to the entrance.

You walk in, looking around you. Dark clouds cover the ceiling, but also rise from the floor; the rain drizzles from above but also gurgles below your feet. Some of the clouds float past you, spinning slowly. The rain comes at you in all directions. It is soft, sedated, ever-so-slightly warm; it makes you want to sleep.

You walk to your bedroom. The flooding is deep. It licks at your ankles, your feet sloshing in drowsy steps. You reach the island of your bed and crawl under the blanket, your wet shoes making a damp spot on the sheets.

'I'm sorry, I'm so sorry,' a voice says. You turn your head a little.

The ghost has given into diffusion. It floats around the room in scattered chunks. One of its arms drifts through the air, the hand at the end clenching and unclenching. You see its legs bobbing up and down in the corner, kicking into empty space. Ten fingers swirl in frantic spirals, and half of a head hovers next to your own, disappearing into a haze of fog before forming together again.

'I know.' You sink deeper into the blanket. The blanket is soaked through, dense with rain. The weight of it binds you to the bed. It crushes your ribs, your larynx; the feeling is calming as a tranquilizer.

'Is it nice, being a ghost?' you ask it.

'It's beautiful. The most beautiful thing in the world.'

'What's it like?'

'Soothing. Quiet. Clean. Like the longest lie-in on a day where no one is coming to visit and there is nowhere else to be.'

'That does sound nice,' you say. You see that the water levels are rising, almost tipping over the mattress. The room is filled with grey fog, humid and dense.

'I don't want to die,' you say. 'I genuinely don't. I just want to nap.'

'I get that,' the ghost says. 'I really do get that.'

The half head of the ghost floats closer, placing itself on the pillow beside you.

'Let's take a nap,' it says.

You nod and close your eyes. You breathe in and let the fog fill your stomach with sleep.

❧

You stay in bed for a day, or possibly many days. The ghost stops the rain but keeps the mist thick and soft. It feels like a firm, heavy hand that holds your throat and squeezes down with controlled care.

Sometimes you hear a phone ringing. Sometimes your stomach aches. Sometimes you need to piss so bad that you think about wetting the bed, and then you do wet the bed. When the phone rings, you wish it were 1995 and that people still owned answering machines.

If you owned an answering machine, you would hear Ben's voice echoing down the hall, and you would find it in yourself to sit up to hear it better. The voice would be saying things like: *Hey, how's everything with you?* Or: *You are forgiven.* Or: *I am thinking of you, and I am always thinking of you.* Or: *You do not need help. I like that you have a ghost. I like that the ghost is always there. I like that you were damaged enough that you attracted one. I like this flaw; I like that you are broken in a way that calls to my empathy and leaves me tender and aching. I love your inappropriate lack of self-control and selfish disregard of our boundaries as consenting adults. It is refreshing and I admire your heart, which some might call repulsive in its neediness, but I find brave and endearing.* Or: *I was only kidding! Let me eat you out!*

Maybe the voice would be someone who wasn't Ben, if it were 1995. It could be friends, if you still had those. Or family, if you still talked to them.

The phone rings, and it is easy to close your eyes and sink into its distant, panicked song and let it lull you further into the damp dark of your bedsheets.

A day later, your landlord opens the front door and lets all the water out. He explains that there had been complaints from the neighbours about leakage, and that he tried to call.

'I'll send someone over. To fix the damage,' he says.

You nod, squinting at him in the harsh daylight, and try to remember how to speak. The water in your hair drips down your face, hanging in droplets from your nose and jaw. The ghost floats down next to you, resting its head on your shoulder. He looks at the ghost, and then at the droplets, and his face twitches. He leaves without looking you in the eye.

※

You take a bath that evening. The ghost asks you to cover the mirrors.

'It's for your own good,' it tells you.

You light candles and place them on the sink. While the water runs, you flick off the light switch. Steam fills the room; you can see the outline of the ghost in the steam, a negative space of a body. Its droplets are something heavier than water today.

You drape the blanket over the mirror, covering it completely. You begin to remove your clothing. You close your eyes as you do so. When you are fully naked, you open them just enough to get into the bath.

When you are fully submerged, you stare up at the ceiling. The ghost is above, looking down at you. Its body cannot contain itself. Its face is stretching across the ceiling, morphing out of shape as it grows wider. Its mouth is the size of a tennis ball, but the hollows of its eyes are stretched across the width of the ceiling; it doesn't seem to know how to be a body anymore. Droplets pour down from its eyes, a steady downfall.

'I know,' you say, and close your eyes again.

'It's just so, Christ,' the ghost says. You hear the downpour of its form on the floor, splatters on the tiles.

'I know. I'm sorry.'

'No, no, it's not your fault. You didn't ask for it. But God.'

'Yeah.'

'It's so disgusting. You're so disgusting.'

You nod. You lower your head under the water. You stay there as long as you can. When you rise, you can see that the ghost has tried to ground itself. It sits on the toilet, its face in proportion to the whisps of what is vaguely the shape of a person.

'It's not just that it's ugly. I think people could think it wasn't ugly. Ben had sex with it,' it says.

'He did, that's true.' You begin to wash yourself.

'But look at it. Look at the wrinkled knuckles. Shedding skin. The twitching eyelid, the browning teeth. Look at the craterous pockmarking of the underbelly. Look at the bulging waves of cellulite rippling across the inner thighs. Look at the hunk of flesh cut from the labia, misshaped, mis-shaven. Why does the spine do that? Why does the left breast hang lower than the right? What's wrong with you?'

'I don't know.' Your throat is swelling up, and your eyes feel too hot.

'And this is the best it's ever going to be. This is the most you can ever hope for because everything will get worse from here. You're going to get older. You're going to swell and bloat and your bones are going to wear down and you're going to hurt all of the time. You'll lose your hair and your teeth and your sight. You'll get diabetes or arthritis or cancer. Your brain will begin to stew itself and you won't be able to remember your address or phone number or name. You'll be ugly and confused and alone and no one will love you. You're going to die so slowly. You're going to be in so much pain.'

'Yes,' you say.

'I don't want that to happen to you.'

You finish washing yourself.

'I know,' you say. 'I know you don't.'

You feel the ghost fall down into the bath. The water rises and spills over the sides as it crowds you. It pushes up against you and stretches itself, pushing out long, dark tendrils that writhe like worms as they circle around you. They wrap you tight at first, but slip past your torso, splashing into the water; it's trying its best to hold you, but it doesn't quite know how.

'What are we going to do?' it asks.

You pull the plug out of the drain. You watch the water twirl away down the hole, escaping into the dark.

'I don't know,' you say. 'I really don't know.'

SQUIRM

Inside of the bath, Dad slept.

The tub was filled with compost, but the level was beginning to drop; at least a third of his length was visible above the surface. Despite this, he appeared well hydrated. His pink skin blushed with health: a hot, deep hue. The layer of mucus covering his body glistened wetly in the television light.

'Where were you?'

The question startled Laura. Dad's eyeless face hadn't twitched, and his long, limbless form remained motionless. 'I thought you were sleeping,' she said.

Dad moved the top segment of his body from side to side. It was almost like someone shaking their head. 'Want to watch a movie?' he asked.

Laura had forgotten to open the window before she left, and Dad's sour, humid odour filled the room. The smell made her think of black mould and soiled sanitary towels. She tried to hold her breath. 'I'm a little tired,' she said.

Dad's body shuddered. Each of the segments rolled back and

forth. She was unsure what the movement signified; his body gave nothing familiar away.

'Do you want me to turn the television off?' she asked.

'I don't want to sleep.'

She went to the tub. 'Good night,' she said, and placed a hand against him. His skin was tacky as split, spoiled pears.

The scent, she knew, would linger on her palm.

Dad gorged himself in the mornings. It was a meticulous process that took between seventeen and twenty-nine minutes to complete, depending on his motivation. This morning, nineteen minutes had passed, and he showed little sign of stopping. Laura sat on the closed toilet lid next to the bath, sipping a glass of soluble paracetamol, and watched Dad eat his breakfast.

She tried to look away while he ate. She wished she could leave during his mealtimes but knew Dad liked the company. She examined her nails, then the rust on the taps, then the sun-bleached patterns of the floral window curtains. She made lists in her head and would sometimes bring a paper and pen to write them down. Lists like: *longest invertebrate lifespan, decomposable organic produce, most beautiful cathedrals in the world, activities to do while sitting down.*

Trying to look away was like running a fingernail against the crust of a scab. The wound was irresistible.

Laura set her glass down on the floor and leaned closer to Dad, hand under her chin. He rolled around in his meal, spittle and compost spraying into the air. She zoned in on the crushing maw, the lipless, teethless hole.

'Oh, Christ,' he moaned. The segments of his body swelled one at a time as he swallowed.

Her stomach trembled, nauseous and tender. She twisted around, picking up yesterday's newspaper from where she had left it on the floor. She read the classified ads and the horoscopes while she waited for Dad to grow full, or to tire himself out. She skipped past all the news.

Laura no longer replied to messages on Facebook or WhatsApp. When asked what she was up to, she didn't know what to say.

Beth never texted but did phone sporadically in the night. On the calls, Beth told her that rosé in Bordeaux was better than in Nice, that her episodes had increased in intensity but decreased in regularity, that she'd bleached her hair until it fell out. Sometimes she called to organise brunches with Laura when she was in town. Beth didn't ask what Laura was up to, which Laura found to be kind.

Watching her father grind into his meal, groaning in pleasure, she imagined how she might reply.

That she had been sleeping in a child-sized bunk bed, feet hovering over the edge. Messaging strangers at two a.m. on Reddit forums, fetish sites, and travel blogs, sweat beading behind her knees. Masturbating with a matted zebra plushie. Pouring cups of coffee; holding them until they grew cold. Shivering in the post office queue, waiting to collect the dole. Feeding Dad. Dousing Dad with water from the spray bottle. Doing this every half hour to keep him moisturised. Lifting Dad from the bath, placing him in the dog carrier, where he coiled around himself, all four feet of him. Opening the curtains, opening the window. Closing her eyes, inhaling the light.

She tried to think of isolated days she might tell people about that could show she was a person, that events happened in her life. Like how last week, she carried him to the park. She sat on a damp bench and threw bread to the birds while Dad spotted shapes in the clouds. Dad slithered down to the pigeons and scared them, sending them flying over Laura's head. How he laughed, and how it was a good day.

Or how the week before, they watched the filmography of Wes Craven in chronological order. Dad curled up in her lap, and his mucus seeped through her pyjama bottoms, drenching her thighs. She massaged his skin and ran a sticky finger down the dip of each segment. She would tell someone that she had wished he could purr, so she could know if he was happy.

She might tell them about the day she held a bottle of salt, and how the weight felt in her hand. That she had wondered how much salt it would take to cover his entire body. Wondered how quickly it would take for dehydration to set in. That she got a calculator, did the maths. Put the salt back down.

Laura stood up, stretched. She set the newspaper down and turned to Dad. 'Done?'

Dad hummed, rolling onto his side. He smiled at her, a gummy, slow grin. 'It's a good day,' he said, and jiggled his swollen centre.

Laura went to the window and drummed her fingers against the pane. Rain dribbled down the glass.

'Laura?'

'What?'

'It's a good day, I said.'

Laura opened the window. Grey mist enveloped her, gritty with petrol fumes. 'Sure,' she said. 'Sure.'

❧

The waiting room was full in the vet's office. There were no free seats, so Laura stood, leaving the carrier on the floor beside her. A stout terrier sniffed at the cage and then whined, backing away from the bars. The receptionist called her name. Laura picked up the carrier and went into the office.

Mr O'Carroll leaned against the metal table in the centre of the room, tapping an iPad with a stylus. A scratch mark ran from the tip of his nose across to his ear. He looked up as she set the carrier on the table.

'I told you not to come back here,' he said. He opened the carrier door and peeked inside. 'Good afternoon, Mr Fitzgerald.'

'John, I'm so sorry about this.' Dad's voice, coming from the carrier, was muffled. 'She didn't tell me where we were going.'

The vet pointed his stylus at Laura. 'You've embarrassed the man. Are you happy with yourself?'

'Can't you just look at him?' Laura pushed the cage forward, trying to encourage Dad to come out.

'What for? He said he was fine the last time.'

'Look at him.'

The vet glanced at the cage briefly. He coughed, then began adjusting the name tag on his scrubs. 'It's his own prerogative,' he said, not looking at her.

Laura lifted the carrier. She shook it at the vet. Dad's body made a gelatinous sound as it was jostled about.

'Laura!' Dad gasped.

'Would you stop that?' The vet tugged the carrier into his lap, wrapping his arms around the sides. He peered into the door. 'Are you all right, Mr Fitzgerald?'

The tip of Dad's body poked out of the cage.

'I want to go home,' he said.

She was quiet in the taxi back from the vet's office. Dad tried to prompt her into conversation, pointing out things like roadworks, bold children, a lone cow in a field. She angled her body away from him.

She lifted the carrier up to the bathroom when they arrived home and opened it over the bath, dumping Dad out on his belly. She dropped the carrier and it fell just as hard.

Dad rolled around to his front slowly. 'Laura.'

'What?'

'Don't be that way.'

'I'm not being any way.'

She closed the window, then took the spray and doused Dad. He plumped up instantly, skin dewed fresh. He let out a breathy whimper, body undulating.

'God, yes,' he sighed. He turned to her. 'Turn on the telly, would you?'

'No.' She turned off the bathroom light. She didn't bother closing the door.

❧

Laura watched her sister impale the romaine lettuce. She dipped it into the side dressing and twirled it across the plate. She lifted it to her mouth, smudging Caesar against her lips, before setting the fork back down. She did this three times in a row.

'Why would you do that?' Laura asked.

'Do what?' The dressing glistened on Beth's mouth, highlighting the angular cupid's bow. Laura and her sister shared the same mouth: a thin, shapely slash.

'You always order the Niçoise. You don't like Caesar.'

Beth shrugged. The movement was exaggerated, like an actor's in a Christmas pantomime. 'You seem to like it. I wanted to try it again.'

Laura stabbed at a slice of chicken, fork squeaking against the plate. 'How's Bordeaux?'

'The women are beautiful, and the men are tall. I'm thinking of having an affair with someone, or moving country. I might get bored soon.' She looked Laura in the eye and pushed a forkful of lettuce into her mouth. She chewed, swallowed, grimaced. 'How's Dad?'

Laura looked down at her plate. The chicken was slightly pink. 'I think this is undercooked. Maybe I should have gotten the Niçoise.'

'Shoulda, coulda. Actually, my hairdresser is doing the raw meat thing. She's lost two stone, but I think it's probably from tapeworms.' Beth slapped a hand over her mouth. 'Sorry,' she said.

Laura shook her head, then nodded, unsure what either gesture indicated.

Beth leaned in. Sunlight caught one half of her, shadowed the contours of the other.

'What does he eat?' The question was a whisper.

Laura scooped up a piece of chicken, considering it. The reddish tinge darkened at its centre. 'Let's not spoil our meal,' she said, and slid the pink meat into her mouth. She chewed, feeling a tendon burst between her molars like a bubble popped.

✺

Dad wasn't in the bath.

She checked under the compost, digging with clawed hands. She hadn't changed it in a few days, and it had blended with his mucus. It felt like egg whites beaten with crystalised sugar.

The bathroom was covered in slime. Every surface glistened like early morning frost. Her feet left gluey prints. The slime continued onto the landing and down the stairs.

He had crawled to the living room, over the couch, up the walls. His secretions slopped from the ceiling. The path continued out to the kitchen and spiralled out the back door cat flap.

The sun was bright in the back garden and Dad lay on the mat of the doorstep, dried to a husk.

Laura looked down at her father's body. Slowly, she stepped over it. She went to the hose attached to the back wall and twisted the tap. Water dribbled then spewed. She pointed the hose at Dad. The force of water knocked him into the door. He cried out.

'Good morning,' she said. She stepped closer, concentrating the spray. Dad's head bashed against the wood.

'Stop it,' he gurgled, twisting away.

She dropped the hose, letting it spray in a circle on the ground. Dad sighed as his body sucked up the water; the sight reminded her of a bulging water balloon.

She sat down next to him on the wet porch. She leaned back

against the door and rubbed her eyes. 'I'm sorry. For the television. It wasn't nice, and I'm sorry.'

'I know. I know you are.' He turned his head towards her. 'Where did you go yesterday evening?'

'I went out for dinner.'

'With who?'

'A friend.'

'I want to die,' Dad said. 'So much. So often. I want to be gone, but I keep going, and I do that for you. And sometimes I think, *Why? Why bother?*'

The garden was lovely in the sun. The grass was lush and fragrant, and birds chattered, silly and sweet as schoolgirls. They didn't go out there often enough, she thought, but she would; she would bring him out here more.

'I'm sorry,' she said.

'Can you imagine what it's like, to have a cock, and then not have a cock?' Dad asked. 'I haven't wanted to fuck someone in so, so long. I used to love steak. I wanted it so rare that I might feel its heartbeat. I ate it at restaurants with friends. I went to restaurants with friends. Do you know what shit tastes like? I do. I know, Laura. They put it in compost.'

Dad slithered over her thigh and curled up in her lap. 'You're all I have,' he said. The words sounded like an accusation.

He raised himself up. He pressed his doughy head into her chest, leaving a damp spot on her T-shirt. He stayed still for a moment, quiet, as if listening for her heartbeat.

In the evening, her bedroom was warmer than the rest of the house. She turned the space heater up to the highest temperature, and stuffed the crack under the door with blankets and scarves. The heat of the bedroom hung thick in the dark, a velveted, sweltering veil that left her body heavy and sensitive, as though softened with fever.

She picked websites at random. She had favourites. She enjoyed the DIY section of Quora, filled with clear, direct instructions and low-quality images taken on Motorola phones. She liked the diverse lexicon of leather kink forums and the fastidious care of medieval LARPing groups, the pornographic sadness of incel forums and the hypnotising violence of their grief. She liked recipe blogs, knitting blogs, blogs for schizophrenia support. She liked the smiling face emoticon, its courageous, self-possessed gaze. She liked the warmth of the laptop on her lower abdomen, vibrating like an affectionate cat.

Tonight, she was in an Irish watersports chat room. She clicked on a profile and sent a message saying hi. She received a message back asking if she was into scat.

(Beth1991): No, not at all. I'm just really, really lonely

(Scatman86): Why?

(Beth1991): I'm in France, away from home

(Beth1991): I don't have many people to talk to

(Scatman86): I meant why not scat what about piss play then? What do you look like?

Laura thought about it. She opened her phone. She looked at a picture of herself and Beth. She pressed her hands to her face and felt the shape of her skull.

(Beth1991): My mouth is very pink, quite thin. I have a small chest, a wide rib cage. My legs are short, and more tanned than the rest of my body. Between my legs, I'm trimmed but not shaved. I have freckles on my shoulders. I have large hands for a girl, bigger than some men. They're cold, but supple. I use aloe vera hand cream every night.

(Scatman86): oh cool nice

(Scatman86): sorry you're lonely

(Beth1991): Thank you. Sorry that I'm not into scat.

(Scatman86): :-)

Laura felt herself growing tired while Scatman86 typed out another message. She blinked slowly at the smiling emoticon and let herself drift off. The laptop screen glowed like a lighthouse, keeping watch in the dark.

✺

She shovelled the compost out of the bath and into a bucket. Each time the bucket filled, she brought it out to the back garden and dumped it on the grass.

She was on bucket number three. Dad sat on the floor next to her, dipping his tail into the water she had left out to keep him moist. He trailed the tail in idle swirls.

'What compost did you get this time?' he asked.

'Bord na Móna, All Purpose.'

'What blend?'

'Green and peat, I think. From Woodie's.'

He flicked water out on to the floor. A few droplets hit her leg. 'It's a bit boring,' he said.

31

'What is?' She lifted a hand to wipe the sweat running into her eyes.

'The processed compost. You should make it yourself.'

'How would I do that? We'd need so much, I wouldn't know where to start.' She had smeared compost on her face. She tried to wipe with the other hand but just got more in her eye.

He slapped his tail into the water, spilling it over the edge of the bucket. 'It's not like you have much else going on,' he said.

Laura paused her shovelling and looked at him. He continued splashing his tail. She couldn't tell if the spillage was accidental or intentional and wasn't sure which would be better.

She lifted the shovel above her father and slammed it down through the centre of his body.

He didn't scream. He was silent, which made the squelch of the shovel splitting his body very loud. He looked up at her, mouth wide.

'Did that hurt?' she asked. He breathed in, out, in. He nodded. Liquid seeped from the severance; it was blood, ordinary blood, which surprised her.

The mutilated part of Dad's body began to move towards them. Dad jerked away. It wriggled closer to him, then edged towards Laura. It hadn't formed a new head, but the wound was beginning to seal itself. It moved quicker than Dad, wriggling with the enthusiasm of a puppy.

Laura lifted the segment. It jiggled in her arms, nuzzled into her hair, rubbed itself against her cheeks. It then nestled into the crook of her neck. She felt the warm trickle of blood from its wound on her throat.

'Get that thing away,' Dad said. 'Get rid of it, please.'

She took it down to the bins. Carefully, she pulled the segment from her throat and held it in her arms. It squirmed to get closer to her.

She thought about placing it in the general waste bin but didn't want to think about it rolling around among the rotting scraps. She placed it into the recycling bin, tucking it gently between old newspapers. She closed the lid, listened to the sound of rustling paper.

Laura went back to the bathroom. Dad had submerged himself in the bucket of water, his body twisted in a tight, intricate knot to fit in the space. Laura picked up one of the new compost bags and tore open the plastic. She held it over the bath and watched the soil splatter down.

When the bath was full, she lifted Dad from the bucket and placed him inside. He remained locked in position. She turned on the television and flicked through the channels for a movie. Channel 4 was playing *Groundhog Day*. She set the remote beside her and sank to the floor. She leaned against the bathtub.

In minuscule movements, Dad unwound. Phil Connors was driving off a cliff by the time he was fully disentangled. She kept her eyes on the television, resting her cheek on the cool, enamel rim of the bath. Slowly, Dad poked his head over the rim. They watched the movie together, both remaining very still.

❧

She opened the watersports website and sent Scatman86 a message.

(Beth1991): Let's hang out.

(Scatman86): thought you were in France

(Beth1991): I'm home. I live in Kilkenny. Are you far from there?

(Scatman86): about an hour I could drive down

(Beth1991): :-)

She sent Scatman86 her home address. She searched through her drawers, looking for mascara. The makeup in her childhood bedroom was covered in clumped glitter and leaked foundation. Crusted layers peeled off in her hands. She found a lidless tube of purple lipstick under her bed, speckled with dust, dead skin. She wiped it off with her sleeve. She applied it, checking her reflection in a cracked compact mirror. She wondered if Scatman86 was handsome, if he would murder her and her father in their home. She smiled at herself in the mirror, her mouth the colour of a bruise.

Scatman86 texted her when he was outside. She looked out her bedroom window and saw a blue car with a man in the driver's seat. She waved at him. She fluffed her hair as she ran down the stairs.

She went out to the car and climbed into the passenger seat. 'Hi,' she said.

'Hi,' Scatman86 said. His voice was high-pitched and gentle, like a malfunctioning whistle.

Laura held out her hand. 'I'm Beth,' she said.

'Liam,' Liam said. He took her hand and shook it. His mouth twitched. 'Your hands really are cold.'

'I know. My dad always says so.'

She liked how Liam looked. He wasn't handsome. He had small, watery eyes that were set far apart like a bird's or deer's, and his pale face was pinched with what looked like fear. He had beautiful, clean hands, with thin wrists so delicate that she was sure she could snap them.

'Will we— I thought, we could go for a spin?' Liam said. He stared straight ahead, out the windscreen.

'All right.'

Liam started the car. His hands had a tremor in them, shaking as he shifted gear.

'I like your hands.'

'Thank you.' He glanced at her. 'You look nice. Like you said.'

'I look like my sister,' Laura said. 'She lives with our dad. She moved back home after university, to look after him.'

'Oh.' Liam's knuckles tensed on the wheel, going pale. 'Is there something wrong with him?'

'He's a worm. I don't really know the details, though. I've been travelling abroad with work, so I don't get to check in all that often—I usually just stay at a hotel, when I do come back.'

They were driving through the countryside. Liam slowed the car as they approached a field of sheep and parked it at the gate. 'Look, sheep.' He pointed at the sheep.

'Ooh, nice!' she said. She turned to him. 'Do you really want to pee on me?'

He jerked back. 'God, no, no. I would never do that to someone.'

'But you said, on the site.'

He shook his head. His eyes were panicked. 'Just me. On me, not on anyone else, not you. That would be horrible.'

'But you like it? It makes you happy.'

Liam nodded.

'We could do it,' she said.

'Really?'

'Yeah. If it would make you feel happy. It's nice, looking after people. I like when I can do that.'

They got out of the car. Liam lay on the grass next to the gate. Laura took off her tights and knickers. She squatted above Liam's chest. 'Like this?' she asked.

Liam nodded, his chin doubling.

Laura smiled down at him. She pushed, feeling a trickle of urine dropping from her urethra, then more. Liam gasped under her, clutching at the earth.

It was a beautiful night, she thought. The moon was high overhead, waxing gibbous. The air had grown cool, and steam rose from the flood of urine falling onto Liam's chest. The sheep dotted across the field glowed softly in the dark. She faced the sky, drinking in the moonlight like fresh, cold cream.

❦

Laura flopped onto her bed, relishing the squeak of the mattress. She twisted the sheets in her grip and kicked her feet. She felt hypersensitive, frenzied as an overstimulated dog. She let out a yelp, just for fun, then covered her mouth. She smiled into her fingers; her lipstick had grown greasy, buttercream-thick on her skin.

She took her phone out of her pocket, smearing purple across the screen as she searched for her sister in the contacts list. It rang out once, twice, three times. The fourth time it went straight to voicemail. She began speaking before she knew what she intended to say.

She told Beth that she wanted things. That the things she wanted weren't always possible, or practical, or right. She told her that she wanted to bring Dad on holiday somewhere hot, though it might kill him. She wanted to lay him down on the beach in the shade of an umbrella, sellotape sunglasses to his face, float with him on an inflatable dinghy. She wanted to make him fresh compost every single day, with extravagant ingredients: oyster, truffle, peacock eggshell. Wanted to feed it to him with her bare hands. She wanted him at her wedding. Not wriggling on the floor but trying to stand, wobbling on his tail to give her away. She wanted the office to beg him to come back. She would dress Dad in a tiny suit in the mornings, tailored to his beautiful, segmented body. Blend steak in the food processor, send him to work with it in a thermos flask. She told her sister that she wanted her to be stable, healthy, to come home for Christmas. To decorate the tree together, place Dad on the top like the silliest star. She wanted to be able to tell Beth what looking after Dad was really like, wanted the knowledge not to impact Beth's life in any negative way. She wanted to find Dad a worm wife. Mostly human-looking, with breasts and full lips, but worm enough to be compatible. She could wrap her up in a bow, leave her in the bath for Dad to find. Sometimes, she told her sister, she wanted to become a worm herself. She wanted to feel her legs, arms, ears fall off in a gush of warm, smooth slime. Wanted to crawl to the bath to Dad, wrap herself around his body, their tails twisting together in knots. They would lose their unnecessary vocal cords, never need to speak again.

But what she really wanted, she told Beth, was to take him out of the bath and lay him down on the floor. Inject him with an anaesthetic, before she picked up a large, sharp meat clever. She wouldn't hesitate. She would bring it down again and again, eight to ten times. Reassure him when he let out that shocked, betrayed gasp. Place his already-healing head back in the bath. She wanted to take the eight to ten segments and place them in a bespoke bassinet, put her head down to nuzzle them, feel their joyful, jumping kisses on her cheeks. She would carry the bassinet to the garden, rock it in the gentlest rhythm. Lift them from it one at a time, place them down on the lush grass. She would encourage them, she told Beth. She would say *go, go, go! You can do it! I love you, and because I love you I want this for you! You deserve the world and you deserve your life, in whatever shape it takes! Nothing needs to be earned, especially not this!*

She wanted to watch the words sink in like water. Shaping the way they thought about her, themselves, the universe around them. Wanted to watch them burrow into the earth, which would part like lips to allow them entrance. She wanted the segments to wriggle out, out, outwards. Wanted only to wave them goodbye, as they squirmed far way.

The heat of the phone burned Laura's jaw. She moved it away from her face, looked at the call time ticking forward on the screen. She put her lips to the screen and kissed it, then tucked the phone close to her chest. It rested there, a warm and small animal, held in her embrace.

⚭

The doorbell rang in the morning.

She went down in her pyjamas. Liam stood on the doorstep, rubbing his palms against his jeans. He raised his hands, as though in defence.

'You left these,' he said. 'Last night.'

He stuck his hand into his bulging trouser pocket. He pulled out a pair of underwear and her tights.

She clasped them to her chest, beaming. She wondered if this was how it would feel to receive a bouquet of bright flowers, a box of individually wrapped chocolates. Her mouth felt sloppy with smiles.

'You should come in,' she said.

Liam followed her inside, rubbing the back of his neck. She patted his other hand, trying to reassure him, but his palm began to sweat when she touched it.

She brought him upstairs. She knocked at the bathroom door, although it was wide open. 'Knock, knock,' she said.

Dad turned slightly at the sound, then turned back. He began burrowing into the compost.

She leaned against the edge of the bathtub, watching him cover himself. When he reached the bottom, he continued to try to burrow. She heard him pushing against the porcelain base with a dull thud.

'There's someone I'd like you to meet,' she said.

The compost rippled. The tip of his upper segment broke the surface, then he reemerged. 'What?' he said.

Laura went out to the landing and pulled Liam by the hand. He followed her into the bathroom, unresisting.

'Dad, this is Liam.'

Liam's face and neck turned red, then the tips of his ears. He looked bright and warm as candlelight.

'It's nice to meet you, sir.' He held out his hand, then dropped it, closing his eyes tightly. 'Beth is a lovely girl,' he said.

Dad's upper segment swivelled to Liam, then to Laura.

'Why are you doing this?' Dad asked.

Liam shuffled, shoes squeaking against the floor. 'I can go. I should go, if you like?'

'Stay,' Laura said. 'I'd like you to, really.'

She sat on the edge of the bathtub, and then lowered her bottom onto the compost next to Dad.

Dad began to thrash. He sobbed, segments bulging with the effort.

'Stop it,' he said.

Laura grabbed him and pulled his body against hers. He struggled, but she wrapped her arms tight across him and held him in place. When he continued to resist, she sank her nails in. She felt him jolt, then freeze as she pressed harder and harder into his flesh.

When he stilled, she began to rock him. She pressed her mouth to his top segment, kissing him firmly.

'We're okay,' she breathed. A trail of his mucus dripped from her lip when she lifted her head. She looked at Liam. 'We're really okay.'

Liam stared at her. 'Right,' he said.

Laura patted the soil beside her and Dad. 'Come here,' she said.

Liam frowned at the soil. Then, after a moment, he nodded and came forward. He hovered over the edge of the bath.

Dad's movements slowed. He took long, deep breaths, quivering slightly. He rubbed his top segment against Laura's arm, sighing.

He turned to Liam. 'I feel so silly,' he said.

'No, no,' Liam said.

'We don't get many visitors. It was a surprise, you know.'

'Oh yeah. Absolutely. I'd be the same.'

Dad moved out of Laura's arms and straightened up.

'I used to be very different,' he said. 'I used to love visitors.'

'Yeah?'

'We used to host parties. Before. Themed ones.'

Liam eased himself onto the dirt next to Dad. Laura felt Dad's body tighten beside her like a tuned string, then it relaxed.

'Before what?' Liam asked.

Laura pushed into the compost. It enveloped her fingers, then her hands. The texture like the inside of a pliant mouth.

She pushed farther, past the wrist, past the elbow. Distantly, she thought Liam and her father may have been talking, or they may have sat in silence. She was unable to focus on anything but the texture of the compost surrounding her arm.

She twisted around and allowed herself to fall deeper, pressing her face into the compost, nudging her nose into the surface beside the two men.

She burrowed down in the earth until it covered her eyes, her ears. She opened her mouth to taste it, the filling heft of it against her lips. The earth enfolded her head with care, its devouring embrace tender and dark.

MOUTHFUL

I've been eating all around me.

Friends notice, their eyes lingering on my mouth and hands for long stretches of time while we sit and talk. I ball my fingers into my palm to hide them and suck my lips behind my teeth. 'It must be hard,' my friend says to me.

And I say, 'Excuse me?'

And she faces her palms out, revealing them with the confidence of someone who has never committed atrocities, and she says, 'We all understand.'

'"We"?'

'Everyone is here for you,' my friend says.

She reaches across the table slowly, like she is trying to pet a dog from a shelter. Her hand pauses close to my face, hovering in front of my mouth. I realise then that she is reaching for my hand, which is at my mouth. I am shovelling pieces of napkin past my lips, swallowing scraps of it down. They are dry and delicate, melting like snowflakes as they hit the wet warmth of my tongue.

My friend's hand retreats, the palm closing into a tight oyster shell. 'Everyone is here,' she says, her eyes now trained on the coffee cup in front of her instead of my mouth. I lick my lips, nod, the napkin clinging to my throat in mucoused layers of papier-mâché. I excuse myself to go to the toilet, where I sit on the closed lid and grasp handful after handful of toilet paper. I bunch the sheets into neat, pliable balls, which I roll into my mouth, careening downwards through my insides in a muted, gentle flood.

On the bus home, I stuff my fist inside my mouth. I bite down on the knuckles, feeling the gummy knob of tendon beneath the surface. Drool leaks down my chin as I gnaw, pushing the hand farther down. The man beside me coughs quietly and glances at me. We make eye contact as I stroke my oesophagus with my middle finger, teasing the head of the uvula in careful, tender circles. I pull my fist out of my mouth. It's shiny and pink, polished with spittle. The man stares at it, then reaches out and touches my wrist, reddened with dental marks.

'You're so different,' he says thoughtfully. He reaches into his pocket and takes out his phone. 'Give me your number.'

He hands me the phone. I lift the phone to my mouth and slide it in. The plastic crunches like hard-boiled pear drops as I chomp, the electrical surges shocking as sour sherbet. The man's eyes track the movements of my throat as the phone goes down.

He reaches down into a briefcase and takes out a pen. He grabs my arm and writes down a number underneath the teeth marks at my wrist. 'My home phone,' he says. He presses his thumb into the deepest indent, feeling the bruising contour, and he smiles at me. I press the stop button and stand, pushing past him. I walk the rest of the way home.

The door to my flat is pockmarked with holes, the wood thin

and porous as loose-patterned lace. I press my face against the gouged material, run my tongue along the surface to catch sawdust from its fragrant wounds. The door tears with ease as I rip the last strips free. The splinters catch on my gums when I begin to chew my way through.

When I am past the door, I think I am going to stop. Because this is my home, and those are my photo frames, and these are my best woollen socks. This is a rock that my friend brought me back from the beach; this is a cinema ticket from the worst night of my life. These are my novelty egg holders, these are my misused sleeping pills, these are my menstrual-stained thongs. Those are my degrees stuffed under the fridge, that is my cactus that I love because it won't die. That is my goldfish, peering anxiously out of the gloomy bowl.

I marvel at my capabilities as I don't stop. At my capacity for fluidity, transformation, change. Some would halt here, take a look around, falter in their path. It takes courage, committing yourself to what is happening. I am a superhero, I think, dangling the fish in the air and dropping its wriggling length into my open, gulping gullet.

The flat is then empty. A few strands of nylon linger on the floor underlay, straggling curls from the vanished carpet. Smudges of paint are smeared across the wall, licked almost clean. I lie down on the underlay, a sprinkling of glass crumbs underneath me. I lift up my blouse and place my hand against my stomach. It is flat and pale, suspiciously innocuous. I try to feel for the shape of my cactus, the hard solidity of the beach rock, but they have left me behind.

I leave in a hurry, now late for work. The manager slaps the desk when she sees me walk through the hotel door, shaking her head. Her painted, pointed nails shine like glossy beetle wings as she stabs the desktop keys. 'I don't even know what to say to you,' she says.

'I'm sorry,' I say, sitting at the other computer and logging in.

'I'm sick of you,' she says. 'Sick to bastard death of you. And I don't mean to swear, but it's pathetic. You're an absolute joke.'

She stands up, wrapping a scarf around her neck. She taps her nails on the sheet that shows the check-ins that I have already missed, and then she goes.

I do try. I do. I put my fingers on the keyboard and I press them into the buttons and when letters move across the screen I watch them, consider their shape and form. There must be some kind of meaning to them, I think. This matters, I think, and I dig my fingers into the crevice of the keyboard. I grasp a button and pull; it breaks free with just a little force, like a loose tooth. I pop the button in my mouth and suck, rolling it around my gums. *Q* to *P* disappear quickly. Then I take the numbers, the comma, the hopeful press of the backspace bar. A guest appears, hovering over the desk. I shake the keyboard at her. *This is important*, I try to say, but my mouth is too full and several buttons spew out. I swallow and wipe my mouth. I gesture to the reception.

'This is important work,' I say to her. 'What we do here matters.' I hold up a piece of keyboard that I have spat out, showing her.

She looks at the chewed-up plastic, and she nods. 'Okay,' she says, 'but I need to leave my luggage here for a few hours.'

She places her suitcase down next to the desk and a small, portable kennel. She walks out the door.

I bend down to the kennel, pressing my face against the bars. A dark, damp snout peaks out, nudges my nose. A pair of eyes that are wise and tired, clotted with tear gunk. It reaches through the bars with its paws and it takes my hand, holding it in its merciful grip. Its bright bichon fur, candy floss sweet.

I leave work early and tell no one. I put up a sign on the desk saying *BE BACK SOON*, then I take it down. The woman's suitcase is open, empty.

My sister's house isn't her house, because she's never going to own a home and neither am I. The landlord buys her daughter a chocolate egg at Easter and hasn't increased the rent, but he might. I walk from the hotel to the pathway of their garden, which he lets them cultivate. The air swims with basil, thyme, sunshine. I slam my fist on the front door, then slam my body against it.

My sister opens the door, and I crash into her. The force knocks her to the floor, and I land on top of her.

I grab her shoulders. I shake them. 'Are you doing okay?'

She stares at me. 'What?' she says.

'I was worried about you.' I lie down on her, placing my head against hers. I press my cheek to her face and I say, 'I am always, always worried about you.'

She wraps her arms around me, hugging me tightly. 'Your breath smells weird. What's that on your shirt?'

I lick my teeth, my tongue too dry.

'Don't worry about it.' I stand, offer her my hand. She takes it, and I help her up. She is looking at me, at something on my chin. I scrub the spot with the back of my hand. Her face does something awful, like a convulsion, and I know she is going to make an observation that I won't be able to unhear, so I say, 'I am doing great, by the way.' I walk to the kitchen, take her French press from the cupboard, look for coffee beans. She follows, watches me from the door with her arms folded.

'Really,' she says.

'I'm so sick of your judgement,' I say. I put down the French press. Then I pick it back up and say, 'No, no, I'm so scared. I'm really scared. I wanted to tell you that I don't feel like myself, but I do. I feel too much like myself. No one should be themselves this much, it's not right. I think there's something terribly wrong with me, and I don't know how I am going to hide it forever.'

'It's okay,' my sister says.

'It's not.'

'It is, it is.'

'I ate my goldfish,' I say. 'I ate someone's dog.'

My sister pauses, unfolds her arms. 'You've been through a lot,' she says.

She approaches me, touches my arm. She has gained more weight, and it is visible in her chin when she smiles at me. She doesn't eat enough vegetables and also doesn't eat at all sometimes for many days and she goes through intensive depressive episodes due to a hormonal imbalance and she dates men who fetishize her size and I worry, I worry, and I think I should do something to fix everything but I am unsure what that thing is.

She leans towards me. She is wearing vanilla body spray from Boots that her daughter bought her for her birthday. Her cheeks are dimpled, tender as ripe, generous peaches. I don't realise what I am doing until I do it and she steps back in shock, holding her face.

I back away and she holds up a hand to stop me but it's bloodied and slippery and I am leaving faster than she can forgive and I am gone.

I start walking back to the flat. The afternoon sun is high in a sky that might soon be utterly cloud-free. I am five minutes away from my flat when I realise I can't do it. I stop abruptly in the middle of the path. A group of schoolboys almost walk into me, splitting around instead and laughing at the near collision.

I look around myself, for shade under a tree or a shadowed alley, but there is nowhere to hide. I take out my phone. There are several missed calls from the manager and two unknown numbers. There are many texts. I look at my arm, at the number scrawled across it.

The phone rings once, twice before it goes through. I talk first. 'Hi. It's me, from the bus.'

'Hello.' The man's voice is tinny over the airwaves, thinned out.

'Why did you give me your number?'

'I'd like to spend time with you.'

There is a sound of shuffling, like he is moving something.

'I saw how you were, with your mouth,' he says. 'I bet you do a lot of damage.'

My hands sweat under the watch of the sun. 'I don't mean to,' I say.

'Don't be ashamed. It's wonderful. Are you angry? I'm angry. I'm angry with everyone. Do you know how much I want to hurt you?'

The phone is so warm in my hands. I wonder if it's melting, the plastic dripping through my fingers like smooth oil. 'I don't know,' I say.

His voice seems to come through my palm, from underneath

my skin. 'I bet you want to hurt me,' he says. 'I bet you want to sink your teeth right in.'

'I don't,' I say. I don't.

'It's okay. I'm a bad person too. I've done terrible things, you know. You can't imagine the things that I've done.'

I'm not a bad person, I try to say, but it won't come out.

'What things have you done?' I say instead. My hands shake, holding the phone so tight.

His breath goes rough through the speakers. I can hear the wetness of his throat, the sound of his tongue dampening his lips. He begins to tell me. After a while, I find myself sitting down on the pavement, crossing my legs as he talks.

The sun beats down on the hot concrete. It burns the skin of my hands, singeing them red as I listen to the sound of his mouth. Like warm, liquid gold, pouring into my skull.

BELA LUGOSI ISN'T DEAD

When Saoirse woke, Bela's eyes were still closed. His nose was pressed up against hers, his cloak twisted under her arm. She could feel his breath on her mouth, stagnant and chill as the meat aisle of a grocery shop. It smelled of fungus, chopped liver, champagne.

Saoirse tried to sit up, and her vision blurred. The room was too hot. 'I don't feel good,' she said.

'I know. We're sick.'

Bela stroked the top of her head; her hair was drenched in something sour, like stomach acid and spoiled milk. 'Disgusting,' Bela said, and began to plait three strands.

Mam entered the bedroom without invitation. She frowned at Bela. He shrugged and clicked his fingers; his body popped like a bubble into glimmering shards. Saoirse and Mam watched them fade to a shimmer in the air.

Mam turned to Saoirse. 'Up.'

'I'm sick.'

Mam pressed her hand against Saoirse's forehead.

'I have work. You'll be here on your own.'

'I'm fourteen. I'm not a baby. And I won't be on my own.'

Mam pressed her lips together, putting her hands on her hips. She looked like she was about to say something. She shook her head and walked out the door.

Mam made her Lemsip before she left. Saoirse lay on the couch swaddled in a quilt, Bela sprawled on the opposite side, legs overlapping with hers.

'I'll be back in a few hours,' Mam said, handing her a mug.

'You forgot Bela's.'

Bela pulled open his cape, leaves and teeth and bubble-gum wrappers falling out. He reached in and took out a steaming mug. He gave Mam a thumbs-up. Mam sighed.

Bela kicked her under the blanket, playing footsie. His feet were bare and cold and burned her skin with frostbite; he left scorch marks on her ankles.

'You're hurting me,' she said.

Ginger hopped up onto his lap; he stroked her fur, the length of her spine. He cradled her skull in his hand. 'Do you know how long cats live for?' he asked, squeezing lightly—Ginger purred louder, nuzzling into his claws.

'I don't know. Ages.'

Ginger rolled over, exposing her plump, plush stomach to the air. Bela dragged a claw down her centre. She stretched her belly up, greedy gut pushing into the sharp nail. Saoirse took a long sip from her mug. The bitterness of the Lemsip made her eyes water.

'Want to watch the movie?' she asked.

Bela smiled, stood. He put the video in the player.

She liked how Bela looked. He was a little ugly, and he was also very beautiful. He had a big nose and protruding ears and a pointed, cruel mouth. His eyes were strange and wonderful—a spotlight always shone on them from somewhere on the ceiling, but she could never find the source. He kept his hair greased back, the harsh slash of widow's peak framing the deep lines of his face. Those lines fascinated her. She wondered what they felt like, the crevices of his forehead, the cracks along his eyes. Before him, she had never seen a man his age so close. He was so much larger than the boys she knew, shoulders wide, long legs towering over her.

Bela usually looked like how he did in the movie, but not always. He was good at changing. He could change into a bat, into a wolf, into a horde of rats. Sometimes he changed into a cat and chased Ginger around the kitchen. Sometimes he changed into other people. He would look like David Bowie or Tom Cruise or Brad Pitt. He'd flash a bright, blunt smile and spin her in a waltz down the hallway until she was dizzy.

Saoirse watched Bela pick up the photo of Dad that Mam kept on the fireplace. It wasn't a good photo. It was overexposed, the face indistinct. Dad wore dungarees, and his arms looked young and strong and sunburnt. Bela put the photo down and turned to her. His face began to twitch, features spasming. His cape and clothes fell away, revealing a pair of dungarees underneath. His head spun in a circle and then stopped. His face was blurred, the flesh whirling and flickering. Saoirse focused on the static smudge expression, trying to see the features; her stomach rolled with nausea, ears ringing. He tilted his head.

'Are you a good girl?' he said, his voice distorted. Her nose began to bleed.

'Don't,' she said.

He stopped. He shrugged and settled back to himself.

❧

They watched the movie when she was sick. They watched it on Saturday mornings. They watched the movie after school while waiting for Mam to come home. They watched it every day on repeat.

Bela mouthed along with his lines, eyes fixed on the screen. His fangs slid out, protruding over his lips, a thin line of drool dripping down his chin. Sometimes he'd practise them aloud, twirling his cape around himself as he flew upwards in excitement.

'To die, Ginger, to be *really* dead, that must be glorious,' he said, lifting the tabby up and swinging her in his arms. Ginger's rusted fur turned grey as they spun, and so did the air around them, shades of it leaking out from Bela's fingertips like a fog over the sitting room. The world turned to black and white. Saoirse looked down at her pink skin, now glowing bone white in the darkened room.

Sometimes they even watched it with Mam, Saoirse sandwiched between her and Bela on the settee.

'How can you watch the same thing over and over?' Mam asked on one occasion.

'I like to know what's going to happen.'

'Doesn't that get boring?'

'I think it's good to know what's going to go wrong.'

Bela nodded in agreement, passing the popcorn bowl across to Mam. Mam stared at it—she looked sick. She closed her eyes and napped while they watched.

✂

Saoirse was eating a sandwich at the kitchen table. Sunset spilled through the window, bloodied light. Bela floated above her in a corner of the ceiling, back straight, one leg crossed over the other. He held a newspaper in one hand, running a finger over the words as he read, whistling to himself. Saoirse heard a knock at the door and went to answer it.

A suited man stood there, shifting from side to side. He was glancing at his watch. In his arms, he held Ginger.

'Is this your cat?' he asked.

'Yes?'

'I was driving past. I hit him, a little. He's fine, though. He's still—he's fine. I'm late, but here, he's fine,' he said, and passed her the cat.

'She,' Saoirse said, but the man had already turned to walk away.

She looked down. Ginger looked back at her, ears twitching rapidly. Something had happened to her skull—it was bent. Her face was all wrong. She was making a quiet wheezing noise.

'Ginger?' Saoirse tried to pet her, but her hand touched wet, sticky fur.

Saoirse called for Bela. But he didn't come out. She ran from room to room, but she couldn't find him. Mam was at work—

Saoirse went to the sitting room and tried to dial the number for the shop while holding Ginger, but no one picked up.

She sat down on the couch, Ginger in her lap. She stroked her fur, slowly massaged her middle; it was becoming cold and rigid. It had the consistency of chilled clay. She reached behind her and put the blanket over them. Her hands shook.

'There, that's nice, yeah?' she said. She squeezed Ginger against herself, trying to warm her up. She waited for someone to come home.

⁓

She didn't know what Mam did with the body. The garden ground was tarred over, with no grass to bury it in. But in the morning, it was gone.

'She put it in the bin. Where else could you put it?' Bela said. He sat next to her on the couch. He poked her side, digging his claw in deep. Saoirse winced but continued writing out sums in her maths copy.

'Where were you? I called for you. Why didn't you help me?'

'You were being boring.'

Saoirse stopped writing.

'I want you to go away,' she said. She kept her eyes on the numbers of her page.

Bela rolled his eyes. He reached over and snatched the copybook, throwing it across the room at the wall.

'It's time to stop being sad,' he said.

'That's not how it works.'

'Yes, it is.'

Bela picked up the remote, pressed the big button. The television flicked on with a light hiss. On-screen: Ginger in the middle of the road, sleeping in a warm patch of sun. The car drove closer. It wasn't especially fast, which made the moment it collided much longer. The shot zoomed in closer; it was gratuitous in microscopic detail. The camera captured a close-up of Ginger's facial expression in the exact moment the cranium made a small cracking sound.

'Please turn it off,' Saoirse said, trying to take the remote from Bela. He held it out of reach.

'What would you have liked to have happened?'

'I don't know.'

'You do know.'

Bela pressed rewind. Ginger, sun, black tar road. The slow, dumb car. The moment before collision, Ginger stretched out her tail and waddled away. She walked back to their house and slipped through the open front window.

'See?' Bela said, and stretched an arm around her shoulder. His cape was damp and growing moss in spots.

'But that didn't happen.'

'It almost did. It might have. It did happen, somewhere.'

Bela pressed rewind again. This time, Ginger leapt on top of the car, sending it spiralling. It crashed into a tree—the man didn't die, but he spilled coffee all over himself. He was late for work. Every member of the meeting pointed at his soiled shirt and laughed. The man was fired. They all threw a party to celebrate after he left. Ginger passed him in the street as he exited the office building and urinated on his shoes.

'I like that one,' Saoirse said.

Bela kept pressing rewind. Every time, the car missed, and Ginger escaped and there was no body stuffed between the carrot peelings and onion skins in the brown bin. During one rewind, Bela reached a hand inside the screen; when he took it out, the screen cracked a little, and he held Ginger by the scruff. Ginger's body was translucent and glitching. She leapt onto Saoirse's lap, nuzzled her head into her palm. Saoirse's hand slid through her skull; it felt fuzzy and cold, like dipping a finger into an iced glass of Sprite. She purred, and the sound was so deep that the vibrations shook the photo frames on the wall.

Bela reached into the cracked screen again. He pulled back balloons, bones, a piñata. He pulled out static snowballs and threw them across the room. Saoirse threw them back, leaping on the couch, squealing when they hit her hair and made it frizz straight upwards. Ginger joined in, jumping in and out of the screen, bringing back gifts; the wings of a dragonfly, the ribs of a crow, report cards from years to come. Saoirse kissed her fizzing paws. Ginger startled and scratched Saoirse's upper lip, leaving a shallow wound; the sting was electric, and the blood was life. Her cheeks ached from smiling.

'I told you it would work,' Bela said. He bit into the neck of the piñata, spilling its sweetness all over the floor.

❧

Their television was small. Small enough that Saoirse could reach both arms around it to wrap it in a hug. The top was covered in dust, and the sides overheated after an hour and smelled of burnt plastic. Inside the box, a bat hovered in an open window, leathered wings no wider than a moth's.

'They're bigger in person,' Bela said.

Below the bat, a girl slept. She was blonde and delicate. Her arms looked so smooth, so round. Saoirse wanted to touch them, feel the lush skin on her own. 'Do you think she's pretty?' Saoirse asked.

'Oh yes.'

On-screen, Bela stood in a corner and watched her, slowly moving in, silent. When he was close, he leaned down, mouth open. The screen faded to black before his mouth reached her body.

'But your fangs aren't even out. What did you do with her?'

Bela smiled. 'I ate her. She liked it.'

'Do you think I'm pretty, Bela?'

'The prettiest, Saoirse.' He wrapped his hand around Saoirse's wrist. Mould bloomed where he touched, green and black spiralling outwards.

In the movie, he came over on a ship full of people. None of those other people made it to England alive. 'Do you really kill people?' Saoirse asked him.

He frowned. He looked like he was struggling to remember.

'I think I probably might.'

'Doesn't that make you bad?'

He leaned in, coming close to her neck. His lips grazed her skin as his mouth moved nearer. The edges of his fangs felt sharp against the rim of her earlobe.

'Do you want me to be bad?' His voice was quiet, measured.

She jerked away, staring at him. He pulled back, standing up.

'I don't have to if you don't want. It's my movie. I can change whatever I like,' he said.

Bela walked over to the VCR player and pressed rewind. He stretched, and then lifted a leg and pushed it into the television screen. One in and then the other. He pushed the sides, pulling the television screen like dough, and slipped his torso inside.

Saoirse watched as Bela had dinner with the sailors. They ate stew and drank beer and laughed at rude jokes. Someone took out a fiddle. Someone else took out an electric guitar. The captain handed Bela a microphone. He climbed the hull of the boat, singing Britney Spears to the sea while the sailors played the instrumentals on deck. In the sky, fireworks exploded, spelling out Saoirse's name. They all arrived in England on time and hugged Bela before they said goodbye. Nobody hurt each other, and everyone was loved.

Bela looked out at her from inside the screen. He blew her a kiss.

❧

They sat on Mam's bed. The room was immaculate, which made it more dangerous to go through her things.

'More fun,' Bela said, opening the lid of her jewellery box. It let out a reedy, wheezing musical sound, the miniature ballerina inside attempting to spin but failing.

Saoirse took the box from him, looking inside. There were sea-shell necklaces from the Sunday-morning market, clunky pairs of hoops, rusted anklets, rosaries in every colour of the rainbow. Bela turned away when she picked one up, making a clucking noise with his tongue.

Under the rosaries, Saoirse found a string of gleaming pearls. She lifted them into the air; they glinted in the light, brighter than a smile.

'Do you think they're real?'

'Does it matter?' he asked. He took them from her, wrapping them around his throat. His Adam's apple bulged against the pearls.

Saoirse opened the drawer next to Mam's bed; inside sat her makeup bag, splattered in ancient concealer. She zipped it open and pulled out a tube of red lipstick. The lurid shade reminded her of the fake blood they sold in Dealz at Halloween, the kind that left stains.

'Will you do my makeup?'

'If you do mine,' he said, plucking the lipstick from her hand.

He kept his gloves on, the silk cool on her face. His hands felt reverent when he rubbed the foundation into her skin. He pressed the lipstick tube against her bottom lip. It was thick, dry. It tasted like Crayola and vanilla. He ran featherlight brushes over the bridge of her nose, across her chin and cheeks. But when he placed the mascara wand against her lashes, she wondered, just for a moment, if he would try to gouge out her eye.

When he was finished, he handed her a mirror. She looked in. 'Oh my God,' she said.

There was another person in the mirror. She was someone older. She was someone sharp and coy and knowing. She was someone who had wonderful secrets. Her mouth was obscene.

'Beautiful,' Bela said. Saoirse touched her mouth and found herself nodding in agreement.

The foundation was too dark for Bela's skin; it left an ugly orange line at his jaw. She aimed for delicacy but felt clumsy slapping the oily cream on his cheeks. The coldness of his skin froze the foundation once it settled, and it fell off in solidified chunks. She took out a pink lip gloss from the bag and tried to apply it to his mouth, but it went everywhere, glooping from his chin and along the edges of his fangs.

'I don't know what I'm doing.' She threw the tube on the bed.

Bela made a hushing sound, petting her arm. He lifted the mirror and looked into it, wiping off the mistakes. He picked up the gloss and began to apply it himself, sweeping in artful strokes.

'You look pretty,' Saoirse said. She sniffled.

He let out a long hum and then scooted closer to Saoirse. His body was vibrating; it began to shrink. His hair grew longer, lighter, a wispy white bob. He ripped off his cape, revealing a gossamer dress underneath—fairy sleeves, thin wrists. His face morphed, and then settled; he looked like the pretty girl in the movie. The girl leaned in, pressing her nose against Saoirse's.

'Boo,' the girl said. Her breath was warm on Saoirse's mouth. It tasted like sherbet.

'What are you doing?'

The girl smiled. She placed a hand at the small of Saoirse's back, stroked the dip of her waist with the other.

'Do you like that?' she asked.

Saoirse nodded. She felt lightheaded.

The girl leaned closer, pressing her lips against Saoirse's. They were soft. They were so very, very soft. They moved against hers in small, firm motions, and Saoirse found her own lips moving with them. The girl's lips parted, just a little, and suddenly Saoirse could feel the inside of her mouth, silken and scalding at the tip of her tongue.

Saoirse froze.

She pulled away, trying to breathe and failing.

The girl stepped back immediately, standing up. She clapped her hands, and disappeared into a cloud of smoke. Bela stepped out of the smoke. He held his hands up.

'Only playing—it's just me, okay?'

'Please stop.'

'Whatever you want,' he said. 'Anything you want.'

⋙

'I found something in the attic,' Bela told her.

'What is it?'

He held up a videocassette. He twirled it.

'A movie. Something different.'

'Which one?'

'A good one. A very good one,' he said, and walked over to the VCR player, pushing it through the slot.

The movie flickered into being; Mam, in a white dress, walking up a church aisle. She was flushed, eyes bright. She walked slowly with careful steps. Saoirse expected to hear the bridal chorus from an organ, but the walk was silent. The movie had no sound, aside from a harsh, static buzz.

At the end of the aisle, a man waited. His face was turned away from the camera. He had brown hair. He looked tall. The camera moved away from him to the roses in Mam's arms. To the train of the dress. To the stained glass, the coloured light on the faces of the crowd. It zoomed in on Mam's face as she reached the top of the aisle. She was smiling.

The movie flickered and stuttered to black.

They both sat still.

'What happened next?' Saoirse asked.

'What do you want to happen next?' He passed her the remote. Saoirse pressed play.

The man appeared on-screen, his back turned. He was walking across a road, a bouquet of flowers in his hands. A car appeared out of nowhere and crashed into him, peony petals spraying through the air. Saoirse pressed rewind.

There was a house on fire. A cat was in the window, yowling. The man ran into the burning building. He threw the cat out the window; it landed safely on its feet. The man didn't run back out.

Rewind.

The man was being shot at by enemy troops. His friend was beside him, wounded. The man was shielding him from the incoming bullets. One hit him in the skull, and he fell.

Rewind.

The man was driving home at night, his face shadowed in the car. Above, a glowing ship appeared in the sky. It shot a beam of light down onto the car. The car floated into the ship, and the ship flew into space.

Rewind.

The man was holding a baby, rocking it in his arms. A burglar burst through the door, holding a knife. The man—

'That's not what happened.'

Saoirse startled and dropped the remote into her lap. Mam stood beside her in her work uniform, holding a Tesco bag. She watched the screen.

'Mam,' Saoirse said. She didn't know what to say next. Mam dropped the bag of shopping and walked over to the player.

'You know that's not what happened,' she said.

Mam pressed the eject button and the player spat the cassette out.

'He just left. Because he wanted to. It's not that complicated,' she said. She walked over to the couch and stood in front of Bela. He stared at her, hissing quietly. Mam looked between him and Saoirse, folding her arms.

'I think this needs to stop,' Mam said. Bela reached over to Saoirse, pressing his hand into hers.

'What? Why?' Saoirse tried to dislodge herself from Bela to stand, but his grip was unmovable.

'I remember what this was like, at your age,' Mam said, opening the cassette. She began unravelling the tape. 'But Saoirse, I'm sorry. It's not healthy. He is *bad* for you.'

Bela squeezed her hand harder; she was going to bruise. Mam knelt down, looking into Bela's eyes. She wound the tape around both her fists. He bared his fangs. Mam turned back to Saoirse.

'This is a good thing,' she said. She pulled her fists apart with a snap—and halted, halfway through the gesture. Her hands hovered in the air, the tape stretched taut between them; it looked like it was on the verge of ripping.

'That's better,' Bela said. He held the remote pointed at Mam's head.

'What did you do?'

'Just paused things.' He reached over and dislodged the tape from her grip, stowing it into his cape.

'I didn't think we could.'

'Why shouldn't we? Why go forward so fast? We're only taking our time.'

Saoirse touched Mam's face. Her fingertips buzzed with static when they reached her cheek.

'Is she okay like this?'

'She's fine. She's stuck. Nothing can happen when you're stuck.'

Bela reached over and ruffled Mam's hair, pinched her cheek. The skin didn't redden, and each strand of hair remained stationary. 'We're not doing anything wrong,' he said.

There was no wake-up call in the morning. She woke to clear, smooth silence. Bela floated above, watching her.

'Good morning,' Saoirse said.

'It's not morning.'

Saoirse opened the curtains. Outside, the sky swirled. Stars stuttered in and out of being, and the moon and the sun circled each other, playing tag. The streetlights blinked in confusion along the empty road.

'What time is it?' she asked.

'Who cares?'

They went to the sitting room, where Mam still kneeled, hand outstretched. Bela pushed in the cassette.

'You stay here. I'll get everything ready,' he said.

'What do you mean?'

'It's a surprise,' he said, and disappeared. She sat down on the couch and watched the movie.

Inside the screen, three brides wandered through a crypt, blood-less faces pale, passive; they moved gently through their dark world. They looked out at Saoirse and put a finger to their lips. They reached their hands towards the camera, gripping their fingers against the glass pane, and slowly crawled out of the TV screen.

They looked different in person. They all had Saoirse's face.

'Hello,' Saoirse said. They smiled but said nothing. They smelled like rich, wet soil. They held something out; a wedding dress, thick with cobweb. It looked like Mam's.

One of the brides took Saoirse's hand and twirled her; the dress appeared on Saoirse's body. It was too big and hung limply from her narrow hips. The brides pursed their lips. They took hold of her hips and pulled. Her hips widened, stretching like elastic; it felt like cracking a knuckle.

Bela opened the sitting room door. 'Are you ready for your sur-prise?'

Saoirse nodded.

'Close your eyes,' he said. She closed them. He took her hand, his claws digging into her palm. His skin hurt to touch. It was like grasping a handful of nettles.

'Open.'

She opened her eyes.

Her kitchen had grown. The walls stretched for miles, the re-frigerator a speck of white in the distance. The ceiling was so high it lay in shadow, bats flitting in and out of the dark. The table had ballooned down the length of the room, and at it sat hundreds of people. None of them had faces, but they all had smiles.

Bela blew a party horn in her face.

'Happy birthday,' he said.

'It's not my birthday.'

'It could be.' He clapped his hands and streamers fell down. A disco ball dropped from the ceiling, and a cake popped up from the table.

'Or Christmas.' Another clap and pine trees sprung from the ground, covered in tinsel. They cracked the linoleum of the floor.

'Or your wedding.' When he clapped this time, the bridal chorus began to play. The guests now wore formal wear and brightly coloured fascinators. They dabbed their eyeless faces with hankies. Bela got down on one knee, holding out a ring.

'Either way, it's a celebration,' he said. She took the ring; it was a Haribo jelly. She put it on her finger.

Mam and Dad sat with the guests, Dad faceless in his overalls, Mam's arms still outstretched in front of her. Saoirse sat down next to them. 'I've never seen them together,' she said.

'We could keep them this way. It could always be like this. We can do anything we want now.' Bela joined the couple's hands together. Mam's hand was stiff, gripping the shape of the missing cassette. Dad's hand looked younger than Mam's, tanned and smooth.

'You know, she was pretty when she was your age,' Bela said. 'I checked.'

'What did she look like?'

'Like you.'

'What am I going to look like when I'm her age?'

'You'll never be her age.'

'What if I want to be?'

Bela frowned, nose wrinkling. 'Do you really want to know?'

Saoirse nodded. Bela reached over and lifted a piece of her hair, gently rubbing it between two fingers.

'Fine,' he said, and yanked the hair out of her skull. She yelped, eyes watering.

Bela was gone. The kitchen was small again. The guests had disappeared, and so had Mam and Dad.

She walked to the sitting room. The furniture was covered in sheets and the sheets were covered in dust. The TV screen was shattered. Saoirse pressed the button of the VCR; it spluttered and then died. She checked inside for the video, but it was empty.

She turned to the mirror, but there was a stranger inside. Her hair was thin and balding in patches. Her eyelids drooped over her lashes. She was missing teeth. When she pressed her hands to her mouth, they were skeletal and dry; the skin was coming off in flakes. They ached, deep in the bone.

'Bela? This isn't funny.'

Their tape was gone too. She searched each room, but nothing was in the right place. All of their belongings were packed into boxes, the cardboard melting with damp. The letter box was bulging with junk mail and bills.

'Bela, I'm sorry, come back,' she called. Her voice was too loud in the silence.

Mam's room was empty, but the air was thick and sour. It stank of rot. She heard something move from under the bed. She got on her knees to look: a dead cat, covered in maggots. There were so many that the colony made a rustling sound as they ate.

Saoirse ran downstairs. Her throat had begun to swell up; she wasn't sure if she was going to vomit or cry. She tried to turn on the splintered television, but it hissed, the plug sparking. Next to the plug, she noticed a black jar. She picked it up. On the bottom, Mam's name was written in a small font. She opened it. It was filled to the brim with a dull, grey dust, fine as baby powder.

A scream was slowly rising from her guts.

She felt something tug at her hair; she turned around. Bela stood there, wearing a party hat.

'Just kidding!' he said.

He took the jar from her and scooped out a handful of ash. He blew it into her face; it was a cloud of glitter and confetti, which covered them both, covered the whole room.

The cloud settled; Saoirse sat on the couch. Bela was on her left, and Mam was on her right. Mam was napping, head against Saoirse's shoulder. She was snoring a little. She was still in her uniform. The movie was on. It was playing the opening credits.

They let it play through without pausing. Saoirse watched Bela abandon the old country, watched him leaving the brides alone in the dark. She watched him arrive in England without the sailors. She watched the girl he didn't want die.

Bela was stiff beside her, sitting very straight. He didn't watch the movie. His face was turned towards her, watching her instead. He reached over, placing his hand on hers. He squeezed her fingers in time with her pulse. Steady, then quick.

The movie rolled on. She watched the men chasing down Bela. Watched them hold a stake above his body, brute muscles aimed just so. Watched the target, waiting. That terrible, ruinous heart.

She picked up the remote. She pressed down on the button, and everything paused.

On-screen, the stake hovered midair. It floated over Bela like a small, curious finch, halting its flight. Saoirse pressed rewind. The stake fluttered backwards, satisfied with its findings.

The tape rewound itself to the start. The title credits tumbled out, and the movie began again. Bela squeezed her hand, his claws scraping her palm.

PINEAPPLE

The smell of hay and faeces hit her so hard it made her mouth water. The hall was semi-lit, red light bulbs glowing dimly in between the cages that lined the walls. Feathers and hair and bone gathered in piles on the concrete floor, soaked with urine.

'Mind your step,' Mary said. Something in the cage next to Jen's head rustled. She peered in, but it hid in the dark, letting out small chirping noises, and then a low, stuttering chuckle.

Mary led her through a door to a narrow room with a high ceiling. When Jen craned her neck, she could see the edges of birds' nests on some of the higher window ledges, white droppings spattered on the floor below. 'Sit down,' Mary said, pointing to the leather couch in the middle of the room. Mary moved towards the easel and cluttered table placed opposite the couch.

The couch leather was wrinkled, discoloured, and frayed in patches, threadbare scabs that looked sticky to touch. Some of these patches had split, and she caught glimpses of the rotting wood inside, vulnerable as a rib cage. Jen didn't want to sit.

'Okay,' she said, and sat down. She squeezed the couch tightly. It was plush as baby skin under her palm.

'Do you have your limits?' Mary asked.

Jen nodded and reached inside her purse, pulling out the sheet. She handed it to Mary. Mary looked over it. 'There's not many hard limits,' she said.

'I wanted to be open-minded.' Jen dug her nails into the couch. She felt something move under her fingertips. Mary pressed her lips together. 'And your word?' she asked, not looking at Jen.

'Pineapple.'

Mary folded the page and put it on the table under a glass of water. She grabbed a splintered paintbrush and rinsed it in the glass.

'We're going to start small at first today. I don't think you'll need to use the word, but if you do, that's okay. Okay?' Mary dried the paintbrush on her leg, leaving a damp stain. Her thighs were thick and muscled. Jen wondered for a moment how the weight of them would feel over her own legs.

'Okay,' she said.

Mary took the glass and a pill from the table. She dropped the pill into the glass. The liquid bubbled over the rim, spilling on her cuffs. She passed the glass to Jen.

'Drink it,' she said.

Jen raised it to her lips. It smelled like burnt plastic. She thought about protesting, but she had ticked off permanent organ damage as the hard limit. She took a breath and downed the drink. It was almost tasteless but stung her tongue; it felt like it had left paper cuts.

'Very good,' Mary said. She took the glass from Jen; her index finger brushed against the skin of Jen's palm. 'That will kill the pain.'

'So I won't feel anything?'

'You'll still feel. It'll just be a little different. Not pain, exactly. Lie down for me. I'll be back.'

Mary went out into the hall. Jen lay down. The armrest was hot under her cheek. When she pressed her ear against it, she could hear something beating quietly inside the leather.

Mary came back, holding a plastic Aldi shopping bag.

'I think there's something inside of the couch,' Jen said.

'Yeah, it was an old piece. I made it for my undergrad exhibition. I'm surprised it's still alive.' Mary emptied the bag on to the table. Pots of glitter rolled out, handcuffs, a saw, a monkey's paw, a foetus floating in a jar, a ball gag, a wooden paddle, ribbons, watercolour paints. The pile grew in size, more than should have been able to fit inside the bag.

'We won't use all of this, but I keep forgetting to get a kit to keep it all separate.' Mary looked down at Jen. She lifted Jen's chin, squeezing it.

'I need to check something,' she said.

The skin of Jen's throat was stretched tight, her jaw held up high in Mary's grasp. When she swallowed it felt like a muscle might rip. 'Okay.'

Mary smiled and then backhanded her across the face, slapping so hard that Jen's head knocked to the side.

Jen touched her face. She expected the cheek to ache, but all she felt was a pleasant, static warmth. Her body was like strawberry jelly, small quivers wobbling throughout.

'How did that feel?' Mary asked.

'Fine. Good. Fine.'

'Good.' Mary went back to the table, moving in a lazy circle around it. She picked up a knife, running a finger down its edge. 'Take off your shirt.'

Jen took it off and lay back down, bunching it in her hand. Mary knelt beside the couch, looking down at her body. Jen resisted the urge to cross her arms.

'We're just going to do a test patch today. Just a small one, right here,' she said, and placed a hand on the thin skin of Jen's stomach. 'If there's no adverse reaction, we'll do more next time.'

'What kind of reaction? Like a rash?'

'Sort of. Sometimes it just makes people feel a bit wrong.' Mary picked something up from the floor: a scrap of brown fur. 'I want you to feel this,' she said.

Jen took it and stroked it. It was dusty from the floor but soft. After a moment of stroking, it began to purr. 'Cat?' she asked.

'Yeah. Do you like it?'

Jen pressed the scrap to her face, listening to the purr. 'I love it,' she said.

Mary wiped her stomach with disinfectant before starting, then picked up a knife. She pressed the knife firmly into the pouch of Jen's stomach. It was a clean, electric jolt, like a glass of iced water after brushing teeth. The cut wasn't very deep, but Jen hadn't realised just how red it would be.

When Mary finished cutting, she lifted the slab of flesh. 'Want to hold it?' she asked. Jen nodded and Mary passed it to her. Jen held it flat on her palm. The slab squirmed, shifting from side to side. The slick, sticky weight of it in her hand made her want to blush. It felt intimate and humiliating, like the time she had held a mirror between her legs to see the wet split of her insides.

Mary placed the square of fur over the wound. She picked up a needle and thread from beside her and began to sew it in. Each prick of the needle was a small, surprising burst; it made Jen think of popping candy.

'There,' Mary said. 'All done.'

Jen looked at her stomach. The square was bigger than she had thought, a long stretch of rich, dark hair.

'We'll get some photos now, and I'll do more video next time.' Mary stood and picked up a camera from the table. Jen saw the chunk of her stomach sitting on a plate on the table, shuddering gently in a pool of red. 'Stretch your back for me. Arch it more,' she said, and Jen complied.

She took a shot from above, looming over her, another from below. She reached down and stroked the patch. Jen moaned, feeling the stroke shoot up her spine. Mary laughed and took another shot.

'Beautiful,' she said. 'Just beautiful.'

❧

'It's a bit horrible,' Oisín said, pulling up his pyjama bottoms.

'You're horrible,' Jen said. She yawned and stretched out on the bed.

He leaned down and kissed her forehead. 'Pull down your top. It freaks me out.' He circled around to her side of the bed and picked up the jumper she had left on the floor, dropping it into the laundry basket.

Jen ran her finger up and down the length of the patch, teasing the split between skin and fur. Each touch sent a ripple through her. She could feel the vibrations of a quiet purr under her hand.

'You should feel it,' she said. 'It's so soft.'

Oisín reached over and tugged her T-shirt down over her stomach. He took the hoover out from beneath the bed and plugged it in. She watched him hoover under the bed, across the carpet, along the panelling of the walls. He stood on a chair and stretched up to reach the corners of the ceiling, as he did every night.

He switched to a smaller nozzle and sucked the surfaces of the bookshelves, the insides of the wardrobe, the intricate contours of her jewellery box and his colour-coded binders. He stopped, picked up the smallest nozzle. He ran a finger down its length. He gripped it in his fist, massaging gently. He licked his lips, then glanced up at her, grimacing.

When he was done, he slid into the bed beside her. 'Is she paying you, at least?'

'Why would she pay me?'

'You're providing a service. A horrible one.'

'She's the artist,' she said, and sank into the quilt. 'She's really good too. People pay crazy money for her mods. I'm lucky she was looking for volunteers.'

'What's her name?'

'Mary O'Mahony.'

He took out his phone and typed her name into Google. 'She's not very pretty,' he said.

'Jesus, Oisín.'

The headshot had been taken in stark light. Mary's face glared out at them through the screen, staring them down. The shaved head, the broad shoulders, the harsh set of her jaw. Jen thought she looked both terrifying and glorious, the way it must feel to jump off a cliff into the sea.

'I think she looks nice,' she said.

Oisín clicked through her portfolio. He started with her early work—mostly hybrids, all animals. Elephant, crow feathers. Salmon, cow tongue. Finch, horse lungs.

'She got in trouble for that one, but it was fine after,' Jen said.

'Do you not think it's a bit cruel?'

'I mean, I don't know. It's just change. She puts them back to normal, after.'

'Does it hurt?'

Jen watched the video on-screen. The finch sat, half-dozing, eyes blinking slowly. Its lungs bulged out from its torso, thrice the size of its body. The skin of its chest stretched like gum with every breath it took, the obscene bubble swelling out until she was sure it would pop. She pressed her hand against the patch on her abdomen. 'No, it doesn't hurt,' she said.

'I still think she should pay you.'

'Why do you have to think about it in those terms?'

Oisín clicked his tongue. He shrugged and exited Mary's website. He opened up Netflix instead and put on a Louis Theroux documentary, leaning against her and angling the phone so she could watch with him. Within ten minutes, he began to snore, his head falling against her chest.

Jen played with the patch, twirling the hair with her fingers, melting into the small thrills it sent up her back. Her hands fell lower, and she found the dip of her thighs sticky and damp.

She pulled her hands away, folding her arms across her chest. She turned off the lights and listened to the sound of Oisín's lungs. His quiet, guttural breath in the dark.

❧

Oisín had left for work by the time she woke. He left no trace of his departure. He never did—she always checked. She walked from room to room, scanning surfaces and ducking her head under furniture as she looked for stray socks, crumpled receipts, a drop of mouthwash or coffee or urine forgotten on the floor. She dove into the laundry basket, wanting to find a used pyjama shirt and bring it to her nose to sniff out evidence of his excretions, but he always emptied it before leaving. The washing machine swirled slowly in the kitchen under her gaze, boxer shorts circling in sultry, soapy waves.

She walked from kitchen to bathroom to living room. He kept the rooms clean by himself, insisted upon it. She thought it should have been a generous gesture. 'I just want you to relax,' he told her one night, stroking her hair. His breath was fresh, his teeth bright in the low lighting of the bedroom. When he kissed her, his tongue was cool and clean as water, absent of taste.

He liked her relaxed. In the evening when he returned from work, he was soft with her. He brought home flowers, fruit platters. He cut the stems of carnations to stop them drying out, arranging them carefully in glass vases. He liked her to open her mouth to receive chunks of papaya and cantaloupe, feeding them to her a piece at a time with his fork. He put on latex gloves to rub her feet, massaging the tight knots of the arch with body oil. Though he was frightened of her blood, he would use a dental dam during her menses and lower his head between her thighs, always pausing to look up at her and ask quietly if this was okay. His hands shook on her hips, unsettled but firm.

The house was precise as a gallery in daylight. It was hard to touch things without panic. She tried to sit on their couch but held herself stiff, conscious of the sweat and dead skin accumulating on her body where it pressed against the suede. She made their bed but knew he would redo it when he was back. She wondered if he could smell where she had touched the sheets, bothered by a lingering dampness, a ghost of residual heat. She washed her hands hourly while at home, scrubbing under her nails and between her fingers. She made sure to rub them after with a rich, scentless moisturiser he had bought for her, to keep them plump.

She hovered in the kitchen, touching nothing, waited for the cream to absorb into her skin. She counted her pulse, counted tiles, counted the seconds and the minutes. Every now and again, her hand drifted to her stomach. She lifted her shirt, let the hand fall on the patch of fur. She grasped it, digging her fingers into the warm, unwashed hairs.

She left by twelve, unable to take the bleached scent of the sink. She went to the library, wanting to check the notices on the public bulletin board. She looked at the contact information on posters advertising life drawing lessons, tango classes, yoga groups.

She thought about writing the information down, but the thought was exhausting. A month previously, she had attended a book club, though she disliked reading. It hurt her eyes. She hated the intimate circle the club sat in, hated the natural way they held themselves. When the brunette next to her asked how she felt about the opening chapter, Jen found she couldn't breathe and got up and ran from the room.

The library was almost empty today, bar an elderly woman browsing the magazine section. Jen sat down at the computers, opened Google, put her headphones on.

The men she watched were always married. Sometimes they were handsome. Eyes bright with youth, excitement, shame. Sometimes they were ugly and resolved. Both pleased her. She liked the tan, supple muscles of newlyweds, liked crow's-feet and sagging chests. Their faces were fascinating. They always looked so angry. Mouths stiff and furious as they plunged into the feminine bodies under them. She wondered what they were thinking. Did they have beautiful wives? Perfect children? Did they hate the women underneath them, their mystery, the ruin of their mystery? Did they hate themselves? Jen tried to keep still as she watched their copulations, her mouth growing dry. Her cheeks warmed painfully, hand damp on the computer mouse.

'Jen? Is that you?'

Jen's head snapped up. Abbie Flannigan stood across from her, lower body blocked by the computer. Jen quickly exited out of the video. Abbie peered round the computer, glancing between Jen's hand on the mouse and the now-empty screen.

'I didn't mean to interrupt,' Abbie said. She was smiling; she had large, red gums that protruded noticeably, and a round, friendly double chin.

'Oh, no, no.' Jen clicked the mouse, shutting the computer down. 'I was just finishing.'

'Are you printing something out? You should have said—we have printers, in the college office . . . ' Abbie shuffled her feet, voice trailing off. 'No one would have minded,' she said, softer.

'I'm researching,' Jen said. She tried to sit up straighter. 'The library is good. For research.'

'Oh!' Abbie said. 'That's good. You're researching! Good.' She nodded energetically with each word. She then slowed her nodding a pace, took a half step closer. 'So, you're keeping busy, then?'

'God, yeah. So busy.'

The two women watched each other. Jen, looking up from the short, plastic swivel chair. Abbie, arm folding and unfolding, standing above.

'Well,' Abbie said. 'That's really good. We were thinking about you, on the course. So it's nice to know you're just very busy.'

The library was quiet. The sound of the elderly woman turning the page of her magazine, the cheap chair creaking under Jen's weight. Under her shirt, a deep, fluttering purr, soothing her ears in the near silence.

❧

When Jen went back for the next session, the easel had been moved to a corner, a black sheet covering the painting.

'I thought you just did camera stuff,' Jen said.

'I *sell* camera stuff. I do lots of things.' Mary pointed to the couch. Jen sat down. The strange warmth of its skin didn't frighten her as much this time. She sank into it, feeling its pulse underneath her legs.

'I'm going to take out the patch before we start anything new. I need to give it back to the cat,' Mary said.

'Is the cat okay?'

'She's fine. I gave her yours for a bit, for fun. Removed it just before you came.' Mary picked up a plastic takeaway container from the table, waving it at her.

Mary gave her the bubbling drink and sat down next to her, snipping the threads that held the patch in place. She opened the plastic container and took out the hunk of stomach. The slab convulsed as it was being sewed in, writhing in the wound before settling. 'Don't worry, that happens sometimes,' Mary said. 'It's just remembering where it's meant to be.'

Jen heard a fluttering sound. Above Mary's head, the pigeons had descended from their nests. They swooped through the air in circles. Their thin bodies were held up on wide, glowing wings too big for torsos so small.

Mary followed her gaze. 'Nice, aren't they? Swan wings. I've got to give them back their old ones soon, but I think they look happy now.'

Two pigeons dropped to the floor, their wings dragging along the ground. Jen wanted to reach out, feel the sleek, gleaming plumage, but paused when she saw the stained feathers that collected debris from the ground, tacky with gum, bird droppings, dark, sticky cobweb thickened with dirt.

'They smell,' Jen said, her face scrunching as she breathed in the damp, sour musk of the soiled wings.

'Yep.' Mary smiled. 'Would you like to try a pair?'

Jen laughed. 'No. They're too nice. They'd be silly on me.'

Mary shook her head. 'Wait a second,' she said, and went out to the hall.

The wings she brought back were even wider than the pairs the pigeons had, beating slowly as Mary carried them over to the couch. Mary pressed one of the wings up against Jen's shoulder blade, spreading it out to its full width. She passed them to Jen. Jen ran her hands through the feathers, relishing their rich, silken glow.

'I can't,' she said.

'Why not?'

'I'd ruin them.'

Jen could feel Mary looking at her. She forced herself to look at the birds instead.

'I wouldn't mind,' Mary said. 'I wouldn't mind if you did.'

They watched the birds rising up to the top of the ceiling and diving down, delighting in the stolen strength of their flight. Jen turned and gave a slight nod.

Mary beamed. 'Blouse off, then lie down on your stomach.' She stood and walked to the table.

The couch felt even warmer against the bareness of her chest. She pressed her cheek against the leather, feeling the dull throb of veins underneath the pillow.

'What did you use inside the couch?' Jen asked.

'Lots of things.'

She jerked when Mary placed a hand on the small of her lower back. The hand was cool and firm, pressing her down further.

'Hold still,' Mary said. Jen felt the icy wipe of disinfectant on her shoulder blades. She wished she could see Mary's hands moving over her spine.

When the knife sank into the tight, tense muscle of her shoulder blade, she became a knot undone. She arched her back, breathing hard.

'Good?' Mary asked.

Jen nodded, her face smashed against the couch, legs squeezing together. She realised she had drooled on the armrest.

Mary began sewing the wings. The repetition of the stitching soothed Jen. Each puncture of needle felt like releasing a breath held in for too long. 'Tell me something about yourself,' Mary said.

'Like what?'

'I don't know. Anything. What do you do?'

'I used to work. I was in a shop for ages. But my partner, he's got a good job, so I took some time out. I was doing a course.'

'Do you like the course?'

'I'm not sure. I stopped going.'

She felt Mary wiping over her back with a cloth. She must have finished the stitches. The heartbeat of the couch was loud in Jen's ear.

'I'm a bit boring. I'm sorry,' Jen said, and tried to laugh, but the laugh was too loud and didn't really sound like a laugh at all.

Mary was silent for a minute, and then she tugged Jen's blouse out of her hand. 'I'll have to cut holes in the back of this. So they fit through,' she said. 'You can sit up now.'

The wings brushed against the couch as she sat up, raising goose bumps over her body; it felt like someone blowing on an open wound. Mary cut holes in the back of her shirt with scissors and helped Jen slip it on: one wing, one arm, then another wing, another arm.

Mary picked up her camera and aimed it at Jen. 'Can you flex them for me?'

'I don't know how.'

'Tense your back muscles. Squeeze them together. You'll feel a point of pressure on either side; relax the muscles on the points where it feels tight.'

Jen followed the instructions and found the spot of tightness, tensing it and relaxing it. Mary sat next to her, getting a close-up of the movement.

'How does it look?' Jen asked.

Mary looked down at footage on the camera screen. She smiled. 'No one is boring,' she said.

❧

'When are you getting them removed?' Oisín asked, hovering beside her, sponge in hand. He leaned into the counter, his posture almost casual, but kept the hand that clutched the sponge poised in the air.

Jen dropped the steak into the pan and pressed it down until it sizzled and spat oil back at her, jerking up against the spatula in protest.

A spot of oil splattered from the pan on to the stove surface. Oisín quickly wiped at it with the sponge.

'She didn't say. Next time, I guess. Could you pass the garlic?'

'You should be wearing gloves.' He passed her the bowl. He looked at the pan and frowned. 'How can you eat that?'

'What's wrong with it?'

'Red meat is filthy.'

She looked at the pan, hummed noncommittedly. The blood dripped into the oil, staining the garlic cloves to muddied maroon. The steak was still moving a little, but it would stop in a minute. One of her wings twitched and then fluttered against Oisín's lower arm. He snatched it away.

'If she forgets to remove them next time, make sure you remind her.' He went to the sink and washed his lower arm. He dried it with a clean tea towel, rubbing it hard enough to redden the skin.

'They're not that bad.'

'You don't have to stare at the stitches. And you're shedding everywhere.' He plucked a feather from her shoulder and held it up.

'They feel nice. You haven't even tried to feel them. Do you really think they're ugly?'

Jen flipped the steak. It made one final attempt to wriggle away, and then its movement ceased.

'At least they'll be gone soon,' he said. 'They're not very practical.'

'No, I suppose they're not,' she said. She ran her finger along the edge of the feathers. Her stomach clenched and her clit pulsed.

'Will you get my phone? I left it upstairs. I'm going to start some pasta,' Oisín said.

Jen went upstairs. The phone lay on the bedside table, facing down. She picked it up; the screen was well polished, immaculate as the day he had bought it. She had gone with him to the store to get it. He had held it gingerly with his fingertips when the shop assistant handed it to him, pinching it between his pointer and thumb until they were in the car, before dropping it in his lap and scrubbing disinfectant wipes against the surface.

She dragged her fingers down the pristine screen, smudging the surface. The lock screen lit up. She tried to unlock it, typing in Oisín's birth year, but the passcode was incorrect. She slid the phone into her pocket, went back downstairs.

'I couldn't find it,' she said. Oisín frowned, stirring the tomato sauce carefully.

They ate dinner in the kitchen together. Evening sun filled the room, a haze of gold. Oisín had bleached the table and counters before they had sat down, and the smell was clean and grounding. The surfaces twinkled in the spots the sunlight touched.

Oisín played footsie with her under the table. When he smiled, his tongue poked through the gap in his front teeth, a friendly, brazen creature popping out to say hello.

She leaned over to kiss him. He backed away from her mouth, giving her his cheek. He seemed apologetic when he saw the look on her face. He passed her a napkin, tapping his own lips with a finger.

Jen wiped her mouth; specks of red dotted the napkin, a smear of grease. She touched the marks, then reached down into her pocket, gently stroking the spotless screen.

She went for a walk in the park after dinner. She asked Oisín to join her, but he was reluctant—his eyes lingered on the feathered tips of the wings when he said he was tired.

The outdoor air felt wonderful on them. She knew, logically, the feathers themselves didn't have nerve endings. That, like the hair on her head, the strands of the feathers were separate to herself, to her body's sensory systems. Despite knowing this, each wave of breeze that passed through them made her shiver. The wind like cold, pointed teeth, grazing the core of each plume.

She found herself spreading them wider as she walked. She lifted her feet higher with each step, almost skipping; the air caught on them on the down step, slowing the descent. She began to jog, trying to pick up speed. She ran, wings catching behind her like a kite. When she couldn't run any faster, she leapt forward, jumping as high as she could.

For a moment, the wings held her up. The air bursting up between the strands of the feathers, pushing them aloft. Her feet kicked out and connected with nothing. The moment stretched as far as it could, like a breath held. And then she fell, knees hitting the overgrown grass of the ground.

Behind her, someone was clapping. She turned. A woman and a little girl stood on the park walkway, beaming. The little girl scurried over to Jen; she was slapping her hands together so hard that they looked red.

'They're so lovely,' she said. Her words were garbled; she was missing several baby teeth. She reached a hand out towards the wings, then withdrew it. She looked back at the woman, then took off in a run. She sprinted across the grass, hopping up into the air between strides, flapping her arms in the air.

The woman shook her head, wincing. She turned to Jen. 'They really are, though.' She smiled. 'I've always wanted to get something like that done.' She put her hands on her hips, looking Jen up and down. 'Lovely,' she said.

Oisín dawdled at bedtime. He was delicate about it; he fussed, adjusting her pillow, placing extra comforters at the foot of the bed. He ran up and down the stairs unprompted to fetch her a glass of water, then a dish of chocolate almonds, then a cup of peppermint tea. He brought each item back downstairs when she was done, insisting she stay lying down while he washed up. When he tried to leave the room to find scented candles, she sat up. The wings dragged against the mattress as she moved, thrilling her spine. 'What's wrong?' she asked.

Oisín stood at the door, fiddling with the bottom of his pyjama shirt. 'I can't sleep with you. With them, in the bed, I mean. I just can't. I'm sorry, Jen.'

'Oh,' she said.

He stepped back in through the doorway. 'Just until they're gone. And I can still stay here, be with you.' He took the desk chair and pulled it nearer to the bed. He sat down, spreading his legs. He grinned. 'Comfy,' he said. 'I could sit here all night.'

She lay back down. 'How was your day?' she asked. Her breath was coming out wrong, and it made her voice strange.

'My day was good,' he said. 'Very normal. How was yours?'

'Good. Normal.'

The wings pushed into her body. She was conscious of their pressure pressing into her back but it was pleasant, like resting her head in her arms. 'Can I tell you something?' she asked.

'Yeah, of course.'

'I went to the library today. I do, most days. I watch videos there.'

She looked at Oisín. He nodded.

'The videos are usually of men. Married ones. I like to watch them.'

Oisín examined her face. His expression was careful. 'Okay.'

'Is that okay?'

'Why do you go to the library?'

'I don't know. This isn't my house. I didn't think you'd like it.'

'I'm not really sure why you're telling me this,' he said. 'It's not my business.'

Jen felt warm. She wanted to throw the duvet off herself, but also wanted to crawl under it headfirst. 'I thought you might like to know. Nice, to share, maybe.'

Oisín crossed his legs. 'I think it's okay not to share everything. I don't need everything. You wouldn't want me to share everything, would you?'

She closed her eyes. The wings twitched behind her, a handful of feathers teasing the backs of her arms. 'I think I'm falling asleep,' she said.

Oisín was quiet for a long time. She heard his chair scraping on the floor, the soft movement of his slippers on the carpet. She felt him touch her hand, squeezing the fingers lightly. He flicked off the lights for her, and she felt the movements of the duvet as he adjusted it. When he left, he closed the door so gently that it barely made a sound.

※

Mary snipped the wings off with garden shears in two blunt cuts, snapping the blades shut.

Each snap left Jen winded with absence.

'It's a shame you can't keep them,' Mary said. 'They were lovely on you.'

Jen didn't know what to say to that, so she picked one of the wings up. It flapped weakly in her hands.

'Should you have cut the root like that? Won't the swan need them back?' Jen asked.

'I can grow out the roots in some water overnight.' Mary took the severed wings from her, placing them on the table. 'The roots in your back will fall out from the shoulder blades in a few days. I'll give you some ointment to quicken the skin regrowth.'

She handed Jen a glass jar filled with a red liquid. Jen turned the jar upside down; the liquid oozed down slowly, thick as mud.

'I'd like to try something different today,' Mary said.

Jen nodded and sat on the couch. Mary shook her head.

'No, standing, if that's okay.'

'What animal?'

'None, actually. Just you. Could you get undressed?'

Jen stood and stripped. She held her clothes in front of her, covering herself. 'What next?'

'I want to get you naked. Not skeleton, but just the outer layer. What do you think?'

'How?'

'A zipper. Zip you out, then zip you back in. We can remove it later if you like.'

Jen looked down at her hands, the pink of her palms.

'Okay,' she said.

Mary moved behind her. The knife was a familiar, cold lick from her scalp to the back of her neck, kissing between shoulder blades, sliding down to the split of her ass and stopping.

'You should tell me something about yourself, this time,' Jen said. She couldn't see Mary's face.

'Like what?' It sounded like she was smiling.

'A secret.'

Jen felt a huff of air on her neck.

'Sure.' Mary was silent for a minute. 'I haven't spoken to my mam in five years. I pissed my pants during a David Byrne concert last August. I think about my old PE teacher Mrs Lonergan when I masturbate sometimes. I really enjoy the smell of my own sweat. I stole flowers from a graveyard when I was seventeen and gave them to a girl who worked in the chipper down the road. I don't really understand David Lynch. I once swallowed several packets of paracetamol while drunk and then made myself vomit them all up because I realised I wasn't really sad, just bored. I think all wine tastes the same.' Mary stopped and walked over to the table. She turned around to look at Jen, leaning back. Her face was relaxed, eyes half-lidded. 'Want to tell me one of yours?'

Jen thought about it. 'I don't think I can,' she said.

Mary laughed. It wasn't unkind. She took tools from the table and went back behind Jen and got to work, sewing the zipper in. She pulled it up, and then pulled it all the way down much more slowly.

'Ready?' Mary asked.

'Ready.'

Mary peeled the outer later off, pulling gently from the scalp and over the torso. She nudged Jen's arms out and helped her step out of the legs.

Jen stood there, dripping on the concrete floor, and looked down at herself. Immediately, she took a step away from Mary. She closed her eyes and crossed her arms over herself.

'Hey, don't do that,' Mary said.

'I'm so sorry.'

'Why are you sorry?'

'I'm so disgusting. You can't take pictures of this.'

'No, no.' Jen felt Mary take her hand. 'Please open your eyes.'

Jen opened her eyes. Mary stared back at her, frowning. 'You're not disgusting. Not at all. But we don't have to take any pictures. I'll zip you back up.'

'Thank you,' Jen said. Mary shook her head. She looked her up and down, still holding her hand, smiling.

She stroked her thumb against the raw, sensitive muscle of Jen's naked hand. 'I really like you, Jen.' She stepped in closer.

'Pineapple,' Jen said.

'What?'

'Pineapple.'

'Oh.' Mary let go of her hand, and then looked at the floor. 'That's okay,' she said.

Jen stepped back into her skin and Mary pulled it up around her. She zipped the back up for her. She handed Jen her clothes and Jen got dressed. Mary busied herself at the table then, picking up the swan wings, dropping them in a bowl of water. She kept her head down towards the table as Jen left.

❧

It was raining. Bulbous droplets leaked over her forehead as she stumbled out of the studio alleyway. A cold bead drippled down her ear, creeping down her neck to the top of the zipper.

She walked quickly. She rushed along the footpath, taking sharp turns around street corners and into empty residential estates until she emerged onto a main road. The gritty vapour of gas fumes was acrid on her tongue as she ran into the motorway, dodging the squealing cars.

She halted at the car park opposite, catching her breath. A computer repair store on the corner was lit up, the mist around it radiating sonic blue. The electronic doorbell rasped when she entered. The man at the counter looked up from his newspaper, nodded, went back to the newspaper.

She took the phone out of her purse and placed it on the counter. 'I'd like to unlock this,' she said.

The man licked his thumb, folded the corner of a page, and then set the paper aside. He picked up the phone. 'Do you have the passcode?'

She shook her head. 'That's why I need it unlocked.'

'Factory reset. Wipes it. You can do it at home.'

'I don't want to wipe it. I want to unlock it.'

He put the phone down. 'That's not how it works.'

She took the phone back, the doorbell wheezing in her ear as she left. Outside, the rain had stopped, the sky clear and bright. A handful of clouds breezed past, light as laughter after their heavy release.

She looked at the phone, the sky's crystal reflection in the flawless screen.

✖

Oisín made pasta for dinner. They ate it at the table, and he grated Parmesan for her and told her stories about work. He made her laugh several times. He washed the dishes and she dried them, breathing in the mellow smells of clean towels and apple washing-up liquid.

They were slow and full after dinner. They lay down in bed and watched *The Office*. They stopped watching and had sex halfway through, and it was good. They both achieved orgasm. Oisín didn't even notice the zipper.

After, Jen turned to him. 'I took your phone,' she said.

Oisín sat up. 'Oh,' he said. His brows furrowed. 'Why would you do that?'

'I don't know if I like you,' she said. 'There's nothing wrong with you, nothing at all. But I don't actually know. And I don't know if you like me.'

He was frowning at her. 'Is that why you took the phone? You think I want someone else?'

'No. I don't think you want someone else.'

He rubbed his eyes. 'Can I have my phone back?'

She got up. She took the phone from her coat pocket and handed it to him. He opened the home screen and unlocked it, holding the phone out to show her. 'I don't want anyone else. I like you.'

He looked small, his face peering up at her from the bed as she stood next to him. She wanted to kiss his cheeks, smooth the hair away from his face, and she wanted to squeeze his head between her hands until he couldn't breathe.

She pushed the phone back into his hands. He lay back down. 'I don't know why you're being like this,' he said. He rolled over on his side and turned off the bedside lamp.

She stood next to him in the dark, staring into space. After a little while, she took a step back, feeling her way through the dark to the bathroom. She turned on the light and locked the door.

She stripped off the items that had remained on. The socks, the sports bra, the ratty sleep shirt. She felt for the zip on her neck and pulled it down. She tried to tug the layer over herself. It was more difficult on her own. The skin was surprisingly heavy and greased with blood, the wet weight of it slipping in her hands. She wriggled it over her head and slipped out her arms and then she stepped out of her skin.

She looked into the mirror, examining herself. Red droplets dripped down her body and dropped on the white tiles of the floor, gathering in dark, murky pools.

She thought about going out to the bedroom. Turning on the lamp, waking Oisín. Twirling around, letting herself splatter on the clean, hoovered carpet, the pristine walls. Holding him and spilling on him, staining his skin with herself. She thought about what he would do, or what he would say.

She watched herself in the mirror, unable to move. She couldn't look away.

NEXT TO CLEANLINESS

'I've been feeling a bit down, I suppose,' Catherine said, 'and my friend recommended you. She said you might be able to help.'

The doctor made a humming noise. He sat back, folding his arms.

'Do you know what it means to cleanse, Catherine?' he asked.

'To be healthy, I suppose? To detox?' she said. Dr Matthews watched her, head cocked. His stillness made him frightening. He looked like the large, looming plaster castings of gods in art galleries, indifferent and unknowable.

'Cleansing,' he said, 'is a complicated business. It can involve numerous methods, numerous factors. Diet, exercise, hormones, hurt, heart, soul, sin, spirit. Cleanses can be different for everyone. We all need to be clean in different ways. Do you understand?'

She didn't understand. Susan had told her that Dr Matthews had prescribed her a week of celery juice and encouraged her to keep a dream journal during her cleanse. She made it sound very appealing. Catherine had looked up the clinic's website and had found filtered images of kale smoothies, medical spanking, possession by angel. She wasn't sure if she understood it all. She had never been any good at science.

'Yes,' she said. 'Of course.'

The doctor smiled; it sent a rush of something warm through her. 'We'll start with the basics. What's your diet like?'

'Ah, normal?' she said.

The doctor stopped smiling. 'Define "normal."'

'Just, you know, food? Normal food? Average meals?'

The doctor was now frowning.

'Sandwiches?' she said.

The word hovered in the air after it was spoken. The doctor left it dangling and looked down at his clipboard. He reached into his desk and removed a beaker. He leaned over the desk, holding it below Catherine's face.

'We're going to try a test. Spit into this.'

'What?'

'It's to test your body's chemical levels. I need to know how toxic you are. Now, I said spit for me, Catherine.'

She paused, and then weakly spat a wad of saliva into the beaker. It dribbled down the side, slow and pathetic. A little spattered onto Dr Matthews's index finger, but he didn't seem to notice. He placed the beaker down and held his hands above it. He whispered something to the spit. The saliva bubbled, changing colour; it gleamed red, emitting a gory light.

'Yes, just as I thought. You're full of toxins.'

'Oh,' Catherine said, and shuffled in her seat. 'I'm sorry.'

The doctor stood, crossing to the shelves at the side of the room. The shelves were a treasure trove of medical paraphernalia: stethoscopes, crystal balls, scalpels, whips, unicorn skulls. He picked up a bottle and brought it to her. The bottle was covered in a layer of dried scum, a sickly, ashen film coating the surface. The doctor pulled a napkin from his pocket and began scrubbing the scum away from the label.

'What is that?' Catherine asked.

'A detoxifier. For the next week, you'll take a teaspoon of this once a day; exact measuring tools are necessary. It will suck up all the toxins in your body. You eat nothing else. You drink nothing else—you might notice slight weight loss. You come back to me in a week so I can examine the results. Is that understood?'

Catherine swallowed. She felt humiliated, a schoolgirl caught with gum. She also felt a little aroused.

'Yes, Doctor,' she said.

❧

She drank the detoxifier the next morning, pouring it out into a spoon. At first, she thought: orange juice. Then: petrol. Then: sour milk. It fizzed as it hit her insides.

On the bus ride to work, she felt buoyant with energy. She beamed at strangers, stuck her tongue out at infants, whistled "Happy Birthday" to herself. She couldn't sit still in her seat. She was sweating profusely; when she rubbed her forehead, her hand came away dripping. The sweat was thicker than it should have been, almost gelatinous. It was like strawberry jelly left out in the sun for a little too long.

She went to the bathroom when she arrived. Susan faced the mirror, mouth stretched in a grimace as she applied lipstick. She smiled at Catherine in the mirror, then gasped, dropping the lipstick on the floor. 'Christ,' she said.

'What?' Catherine met Susan's eyes in the mirror, and then she saw herself. The reflection looked like her, but much slimmer. Catherine waved and the doppelgänger did the same. They grinned at each other.

She received many compliments during the first hour of her shift. Coworkers passing her desk stopped in their tracks, praising her light shape, her svelte figure, her healthy, glowing skin. She thanked them, wiping the sweat from under her eyes, where it gathered in pools, solidifying as it cooled.

She cleaned her hands in between typing emails, wiping her fingers with a tissue each time she pressed send. Despite her efforts, sweat quickly built up on the keyboard, oozing between the cracks. It had a tacky texture like half-dry glue and left the keys malfunctioning in spots. The backspace button grew so gummy that it stiffened, impossible to use. She decided to take a coffee break and find Susan.

'Are you ill?' Susan asked, passing her a mug in the break room. 'You're thinner than this morning. You should take better care of yourself.'

'I don't know,' Catherine said. She tugged at her blouse, conscious of the growing damp spots. Jellied clumps of sweat fell farther down the split of her breasts, wedging under the band of her bra. 'I was thinking it might be the cleanse.'

Susan frowned. 'Why would you think that?'

'Did you find it, I don't know, a bit odd?'

'I loved it. They can be hard, but it's all about discipline, isn't it? Why, are you struggling with that?'

Catherine put the mug down on the counter. A glob fell from

her index finger, spotted with flecks of red like a bloodied egg yolk. At the tip of her index finger, there was a clean piece of bone shining through.

'No, it's fine,' Catherine said. 'You're right. Just ill. Maybe Rob will let me take the day off.'

Rob did let her take the day off. 'You look awful,' he said. 'Did something happen? Is this about the other night? Is this because of me?'

'What do you mean?'

'Catherine, look at yourself. You're not well.'

Catherine looked down. Her body had grown smaller, clothes slipping off her frame. She lifted a hand; all the flesh had dripped away below the wrist, her skeleton now exposed.

'I'm on a cleanse,' she said.

'That might help you, then. I think you should take some time off. You're going to make your coworkers uncomfortable.' Rob stared at a spot next to her face, not meeting her eyes. A glob fell from her other hand, hitting the linoleum of the floor with a dull splatter. Catherine nodded and left.

❧

She tried to call the clinic after work. When she heard the cool, distant tone of the receptionist's voice asking her to explain the issue, she looked down at herself and found she couldn't say the words aloud. She breathed out an apology and hung up.

She opened Instagram and quickly found the doctor's account: yoga poses, quinoa bowls, bloodletting circles, medical conferences. In many of the posts, he was with beautiful people. She wondered which ones he had slept with. He could have any of them. He was beautiful himself. He looked like a soldier in the photos, or what she thought a soldier would look like. Strong and competent and heartless.

Catherine went to her bedroom and stripped. Her tights were bulging with the sweat. Or what probably wasn't sweat at all. She held the tights above her face, feeling the weight of the substance filling them; when she squeezed, it felt like gripping the blubbery underbelly of a puppy.

The rest of her clothes were filled too, bulbous as water balloons. She looked into her mirror; her body had dripped completely clean. Her skeleton was so bright it looked like she had been dunked in bleach. The skull was the worst part. The eyes had remained, but nothing else. She wasn't sure why; she thought about searching WebMD. She ran her hands along the hard smoothness of herself and tapped the bones of her rib cage. She almost expected them to ring out like a xylophone, clear and sweet, but all they made was a hollow thud.

❧

Dr Matthews opened the door. His eyes scanned over her. His expression didn't change.

'That's unfortunate,' he said, and gestured for her to enter. She stepped inside, arms crossed self-consciously. She had dressed in layers and sunglasses to cover the worst of it. The doctor moved to sit at his desk, and she followed suit.

'So, is this bad?' She took off her sunglasses; she didn't want to be rude.

'Not bad. Not good either. The toxins are gone, for now, but it means you had nothing else left,' he said, and picked up his clipboard. 'Do you feel empty, Catherine?'

'Pardon?'

'Physically speaking. Or spiritually. Do you feel empty? Incomplete? Hungry for something more? Do you feel like you're missing something inside of you?'

Catherine moved her hand to the space where her stomach once was. 'Yeah, maybe,' she said.

The doctor smiled, approving, and ticked a box on his clipboard. 'That's okay,' he said. 'It's okay to be hungry. Food is a healer, Catherine. It's a kind of magic. We all need to feel full.'

He opened a drawer in his desk and removed a dish bearing a metal cover and cutlery. 'You're going to eat this,' he said, 'and you're going to feel so full, Catherine. Bursting.'

She lifted the lid: a slab of raw meat on a plate.

'Steak's better for you blue,' the doctor said. 'Eat up.'

She cut into the steak. Blood oozed from the cut, a steady flow. Looking closely, she could see the steak expanding out and in, shuddering with life. She hesitated, lifted the piece to her mouth, and bit. Her eyes fluttered as warm red waves of pleasure flooded into her.

'Good, isn't it?' the doctor said. He was sitting back with his hands behind his head, smiling.

She looked down at herself. Flesh was growing from her bones like mould, tissue forming in clumps at her joints. The tissue wriggled, spreading out, merging to form clumps of muscle, tendons, trickles of veins flowing over the length of her skeleton. Another bite and organs bloomed, blossoming up from her rib cage and spreading out across the raw, exposed plains of her torso. Her heart inflated, rising up. It gave a nervous jerk, stuttering out a few syncopated beats before remembering its rhythm. She swallowed more of the steak and skin grew, translucent and thin as wet paper.

'What kind of meat is this?' she asked.

The doctor just grinned.

She abandoned the fork, picking up the steak with her hands. Her body had grown back, but the taste. Christ, the taste. She couldn't stop eating. Silken at the back of her throat, like melted chocolate. Warm and rich and sweet too. But not chocolate. Not even really food, or even really taste. The weight of it in her mouth felt like the heat of her blanket on cold mornings, heavy and suffocating and irresistible.

'Someone's a glutton.'

Catherine startled, dropping the steak. It landed on her stomach, which stretched out in front of her, immense. She couldn't see the doctor behind it. Her stomach bulged over the desk, spilling down the side of the wood, which creaked under its weight. Inspecting further, she could see the doctor buried under the flab of her belly. He squeezed his hands out and lifted one of the rolls of fat, burrowing his head forward with a wiggling motion until it was free.

'So,' he asked, 'do you feel full?'

'I feel sick.'

'That's a pity.'

He squirmed underneath her stomach—an arm shot out, a syringe in hand.

'Hold still,' he said, and stabbed her stomach. It burst like an overgrown blister, letting out a hollow pop of air. Nothing splattered out—she was empty. She wondered how that was possible. Were other patients empty like her? Were they full? What were they filled with? She wanted to ask the doctor but didn't want to sound ignorant.

The doctor cut away the dead skin, bandaged the wound. His hands felt firm and certain as they moved against her torso. When he had finished, his eyes locked on hers.

'Come back to me tomorrow. You'll have healed by then.'

❧

'How often do you achieve orgasm, Catherine?' Dr Matthews asked.

He stretched on a yoga mat on the floor of his office, practising downward-facing dog. A long shape wagged from beneath the back of his trousers, distracting Catherine.

'Excuse me?'

'Orgasm plays a powerful part in our well-being. It can make or break a cleansing. How often do you climax?'

'Ah, regularly?'

The doctor shifted to tree pose. His arms stretched out to the ceiling, leaves sprouting from the pores of his skin.

'By "regularly," do you mean excessively? Excess can be isolating. Damaging, even. Granted, not always the cause, but almost definitely a symptom. Did you know that chronic masturbators are often suicidal? Einstein once argued that we masturbate as a way to run from death—those who run more, run faster, are often those who feel closer to the void, so to speak.'

'I don't— I have lovers.'

'So? Do your lovers make you come? Can you come in general? Are you afraid to? Are you terrified of letting go? Do you believe yourself to be undeserving of love? Are you a bad person, Catherine?'

The doctor bent his limbs to a half-moon pose. His skin began to shine, emitting a dazzling, milky light. She stared at the light until the rest of the room faded to shadow, blinding herself with its brightness.

'What?' she said. She couldn't think. She wanted to bathe in his glow. The doctor's moonlight darkened as he sighed.

'You are prolonging the process by not being open. Your opacity indicates that there is something deeply problematic with regards both to you and your sex life,' he said. He stepped off the mat, and the yoga marks faded away. The leaves fell in piles to the floor, his celestial skin dimmed to flesh. He gestured towards the medical bed at the back of the room.

'Lie down there. Back straight. Legs spread. Now,' he said.

She tried not to shake as she walked to the bed. He followed her, standing between her legs. She felt faint, looking down at him through them.

'This is not a place of shame, but it is a place of healing. Will you let me fix you?'

'Of course. I'm sorry.'

'For the next week, you aren't going to orgasm. I'm going to close you up, to make sure. At the end of the week, you spit in a beaker. The week after that, you achieve orgasm every night. You spit in a beaker at the end. You come back in two weeks with the beakers, we compare their varying toxicity levels. Clear?'

'How are you going to close me up?'

The doctor reached behind her ears. He produced a pill and a bottle of water from behind them. He winked.

'Take this. Then, lift your hips, and snap your legs shut. Check the results when you're home. It's all very safe. It's often used as a contraceptive in Sweden.'

She followed his instructions. She felt a tightening in her lower body. She winced.

'Don't forget to sort payment at reception,' Dr Matthews said, pointing to the door.

❦

She stripped in the bathroom once she was home, goose-bumping in the cold. She sat on the cool tiles in front of the long mirror, opened her legs, and looked.

She thought it would look as friendly and clean as a Ken doll, chirpy with asexual smoothness. But it looked painful and ugly, like a pair of hands locked together with superglue.

She rang Susan on Tuesday evening after drinking a large glass of wine, to check if her break had caused disruption. Susan reassured her that her absence hadn't affected anyone. This didn't surprise Catherine. She wasn't really sure what her job was. She thought she might be in marketing but had never received a firm answer from Rob.

'But we do miss you,' Susan said. 'Come back!'

'I'm not allowed.'

'After the cleanse, I mean. When you're feeling better.'

Catherine swirled the stem of the glass, spilling a little wine on her bed. 'Susan, what did you think of Dr Matthews? Did he really help you?'

'I thought he was brilliant. Tough, but brilliant. Kind of sexy too. Why, are you finding him helpful?'

Catherine flicked her glass. She was disappointed when it didn't crack. 'He's great. Really great,' she said.

On the seventh day, she felt a rush of release, like unclenching a jaw that she hadn't known she was tensing. She spat into a beaker, leaving it on a shelf in the bathroom.

That evening, she sent Rob a picture of her tits and he arrived within half an hour, looking guilty and excited. He spent four minutes jabbing her urethra, pinched her nipples twice, and then slipped on the condom. He moved his hips in quick, shallow pumps.

'Yeah, you fucking cunt,' he said, speeding up.

'What?' Catherine said, but he had already begun to come. After he left, she finished herself off while thinking about Dr Matthews's hands.

When she was done, she walked into the kitchen, not turning on the lights. She washed her hands under the tap. She made herself a bowl of cereal and ate it in the dark, hovering over the sink. The tiles of the floor numbed the soles of her feet with cold. The drip of the tap was loud in the silence.

*

'Place the beakers on the desk for me, Catherine,' the doctor said. He was hovering in the air above the desk, legs crossed, arms outstretched. Numerous candles were balanced along his shoulders and arms, all lit. Catherine took the two beakers from her purse and placed them down. She hesitated, and then sat down. The doctor hadn't yet looked at her.

Dr Matthews let out a long hum and began to slowly float down to his seat. The candles remained hovering in the air.

'Right, then,' he said, rubbing his hands together and leaning over the beakers. He began to whisper to them. Once again, the saliva in both turned a bright, glowing red. Identical.

The doctor frowned, and the flames of the candles flickered out.

'That can't be right,' he said. He whispered again, but the saliva stayed the same. He looked up at Catherine, and her stomach jumped.

'How are you feeling?' he asked.

'Fine, thanks.'

'I meant in regard to the experiment. Did it have any effects? Did the first week leave you calm, peaceful, clear? Or agitated? Did the second week leave you sated, rejuvenated? Or perhaps unsatisfied, lonely, dejected? How did they make you feel?'

'Well, tense, the first week, I suppose.'

The doctor rolled his eyes. A candle fell out of the air, hitting the floor.

'Not the physical results. I mean how you feel. Feel, Catherine. Your emotions. Heart, spirit, energy. How did the two weeks make you feel? Was there a difference?'

Catherine thought for a moment and shook her head. 'I felt the same both weeks, for the most part.'

The doctor exhaled through his nose, and all the candles

dropped with a clatter. One barely missed Catherine's skull. She could see the annoyance on the doctor's face. She looked to a spot behind his head, a poster of a woman eating salad, head thrown back in mirth. Beneath it, the words: *LIVE, LAUGH, LOVE.*

The doctor breathed out.

'Right,' he said. He clapped his hands. A plastic container filled with green liquid and a straw appeared on the desk. He handed it to her.

'What is this?' she asked.

'A kale and banana smoothie.'

'Are you serious?'

'Catherine, I only help those who are willing to help themselves,' he said. He stood and began picking up the candles, shoving them somewhere inside his lab coat.

'You're as toxic as ever, which shouldn't even be possible. The chemical levels are identical to week one. Do you realise most people take a week, at most? A week with me, and they're clean. They're happy. But you. It's like you're choosing to be unhappy.' He stopped, ran a hand through his hair. He whistled, and all at once, the remaining candles on the floor melted to wax.

'Drink the smoothie. Drink one each morning; they're good for digestion. Meditate. Get plenty of exercise. Get air, get sun. Smile. Do something that scares you. Do something you love. Say "I love you." Embrace your life, embrace your career. Practise gratitude. Pet a dog. Dance in the rain. Cut off negative people. Update your Twitter. Tell everyone about your day. Eat a salad. I don't know, do it all. Do none of it. But you've got to at least try to be happy,

Catherine. Right now, I don't think you're trying at all. You're wasting your time and you're wasting mine. If you aren't going to try, I can't help you.'

Catherine stared at her hands, clenched in her lap.

'I'm sorry,' she said.

'Take the smoothie and come back next week.'

She picked up the smoothie. She stood from the chair and crossed the room, head down as she left.

The next morning, she blitzed kale and banana in the blender.

She drank green smoothies every day for a week. She rang her office and asked to come back to work. She slipped out at five a.m. to run around the block, to meditate, to examine the colours of the rising sun—pale amber to burnt orange to so much red, a sky the colour of a butcher's window.

She thought about the sky, about the world. She wrote her thoughts in a Bullet Journal. She contemplated gratefulness. She wrote the words 'I am grateful' over and over for thirty pages. She grated carrots and peppers, mixed vinaigrettes, threw her head back and laughed at her coworkers' jokes while eating colourful salads.

'You have a beautiful smile. I appreciate your presence in my life,' she told Susan while printing pictures of baby animals to stick above her computer.

She cleaned her apartment, bleached the floors. She tossed the dresses that didn't fit. She packed away all the half-read novels she wasn't going to finish and gave them to a charity shop. She volunteered for an evening at the dog shelter, stroked the fur of the blind, limping greyhound, anointed herself with the soured smell of canine.

She stared at the ceiling at night and thought about how to be happy. She listened to podcasts about self-enlightenment and Alan Watts and focused on her breathing. She lay in the dark until she dropped off to sleep.

❧

'You must understand, there's only so long this can go on,' Dr Matthews said.

Catherine nodded, trying to concentrate. The doctor was usually clean-shaven, but he had allowed himself to roughen this week, stubble framing his lower face. It fascinated her. She couldn't stop looking at his mouth.

'There are other types of cleanses we could try if we had time. Gravity recentring, sterile flagellation, psycho diving, keto. But it's outside of the price bracket we established,' he said, filling out a form.

'So, we're done?' she asked. She felt dazed, far away from her body.

'Not quite. I think I'd like to try one more thing. Have you ever had a tooth extracted?' he asked.

She nodded. She prodded the backs of her gums with her tongue, feeling for the tender spot.

The doctor stroked the stubble under his lower lip. 'It's a similar process, this kind of extraction. Philosophically speaking, that is.' He pointed at the bed in the corner. His nails looked smooth, filed in clean curves. 'Lie down,' he said.

She walked over to the bed. Dr Matthews followed her. He leaned over her, taking out a syringe. This close, Catherine could smell his skin. She felt the pinch of the syringe in her arm.

He peered down at her face, looking into her eyes.

'How'd that feel?' he asked.

She stretched up and placed a kiss on his mouth. His lips were pliant and dry, and his stubble scratched her chin.

He stepped back. He frowned.

'You are not interesting to me, and I do not find you physically attractive,' he said.

'Oh,' she said.

'Right, extraction,' he said, and moved back to his desk, opening a drawer. He removed a pair of rubber gloves.

'Upon examination of your reactions to different forms of cleansing, I have concluded that purification of toxins is not enough. You will, as you have already done, continue to produce more. This indicates that there is something toxic built into your system.'

He pulled the gloves on with a tight snap. 'To put it simply, there is something wrong with you. I'm going to pull that wrongness out.'

'How do we do it?'

'The anaesthetic will have kicked in by now, so we'll have you lie back down.'

Catherine did as she was told. Dr Matthews was right: the anaesthetic was working—her head was filling with cotton balls and softness.

'Open wide and say "ah."'

'Ah,' she said, opening her mouth. The doctor put his fingers in her mouth—the powdery plastic taste of latex was comforting. He grabbed her lower gums and pulled hard. It should have hurt, but it didn't. Her jaw felt like taffy, stretching farther than she'd thought possible. It fell down and down until she could feel her bottom lip against her collarbones.

The doctor pulled a small flashlight from inside his lab coat and pointed it into her mouth. He peered into her throat, into her guts.

He hummed. 'Oh, oh yes. There it is.' He clicked his tongue and put the torch away. He pushed his fingers farther into her mouth, past the knuckles, slipping his fist inside her.

'Breathe through your nose,' he said, and slid his fist down her throat.

She breathed sharply in through her nostrils, braced for pain. But there was no pain. The fist was full and firm but unimportant. Her body was gaseous and impermanent as an afterthought.

The doctor's fist moved farther through the cloud of her insides and stopped somewhere in her stomach. The hair of his arm tickled a little against the walls of her throat. The hand made a sudden movement, jerking against her side. Then, all at once, the doctor was ripping it back up and out of her.

Catherine spluttered as the fist pulled out of her mouth, saliva dribbling down her chin. She sat up, clutching at her jaw, which swung loosely against her chest. The doctor was holding something bloody in his hands. It wriggled in his grip. *What is that?* Catherine tried to say, but her jaw was too stretched for speech.

The thing was convulsing, spasming in the doctor's hands. It was emitting a high-pitched keening sound, desperate and ugly. She thought of drowning puppies. Dr Matthews lifted the thing and examined it—it seemed to have limbs, a torso, a throat, which he held it by. She stood, looked closer. It had eyes. It had huge, horrified eyes, and it was screaming. Dr Matthews turned to her, still dangling the creature in the air by the throat. Its bloodied paws tore feebly at his fingers. He didn't notice.

'Sit, sit,' he said, gesturing with the extraction. Its body flopped up and down with the motion, red fluid splattering on the doctor's coat. The liquid seemed to leak from the creature itself, flowing directly from its pores. The doctor scowled at the spray, rolled his eyes to the roof.

She sat down on the bed. She watched as the doctor went to his shelves, the creature swinging in his grasp like a shopping bag. Its screams lowered to a whine as its airflow was cut off by his fist. He took a metal tray from the shelf and placed it on his desk before dropping the creature into it. It landed with a moist, heavy thud.

He turned around. 'Just give that a few minutes,' he said, wiping his hand on his coat. He came towards her. He reached down, putting the hand he had wiped under her chin to lift her jaw from her lap. His fingers felt slippery, the residue on them warm. He pressed his thumbs firmly into the flesh, pushing upwards. Catherine registered pressure and heard a loud, sharp click.

The creature whimpered in the tray. 'Ignore that.' The doctor pulled his chair over. He picked up his clipboard and sat down, loosened his tie.

'So, there are some exit questions I'm going to ask you,' he said. 'You can write out the answers. Look, you can have a turn with this!' He passed her the clipboard, eyes crinkling; she thought that he had never been more pleased.

'What is that thing?' Her words were slurred; her tongue felt heavy, mouth flooded with saliva. The doctor put his finger to his lips, then made a writing motion.

'What's your relationship like with your mother?' he asked.

When she opened her mouth, he shook his head, pointed at the clipboard. She looked down at it. She answered the question. He asked another question. She answered. Asked. Answered. The pen wobbled, her responses a blue, shuddering scratch. Her jaw throbbed, throat raw and hollow.

He took the clipboard from her without warning. He read through the answers. A furrow appeared on his brow. He looked up at her. 'I think you might be confused.'

'Yes, I am very confused,' she said. 'What are you going to do with the extraction?'

'Oh, it'll expire in a minute.' He glanced over at his desk. He then did a double take, neck craning around. He stood, chair scraping loudly, and rushed to his desk. He picked up the metal tray, peering into it. He lifted it higher and inspected the bottom.

'Is everything all right?' Catherine asked.

The doctor put down the tray. He placed his hands on his hips, looking across the floor. 'Y-e-e-e-s,' he said slowly, drawing out the vowel. 'Yes, it's all right.'

He ducked down under the desk. 'Could you have a look around you, in that area?' His voice was muffled. She could see his hands and knees on the ground as he crawled around on the tile.

Catherine looked. Her feet, the chairs. The shelves, the posters. The white walls, luminous—bar a spot near the bottom smudged with maroon. Another smudge, smeared across the desk. The doctor's head appeared under the desk. 'There!' he said, eyes wide. 'Grab it!'

She spun, arms flailing. 'Where?'

The doctor scrambled backwards, banging his head on the wood. 'The door, get the door!'

The door, a crack widening as it creaked ajar. A small, gory figure, darting through the crack.

Catherine ran to the door, yanking it open. The infantile form waddled speedily through the hallway, past the reception. With each quick step, it seemed to grow, its short, plump body like a toddler, then a gangly teen. Its body lengthened and thinned, arms stretched like chewing gum as they windmilled in the air, legs elongating in elasticated strides.

She unfroze and tried to chase after it, but it was too fast, leaping out the building entrance and running off down the road. It left a trail of ooze in its wake as it ran into the crowds on the street. A few stopped and stared as it darted past, but it quickly made its way past the throng, disappearing from view.

Catherine returned to the office. 'It got away,' she said.

The doctor blew air out of his mouth. 'Unfortunate,' he said. He sat at the desk, wiping the smudge with his coat sleeve.

'What do we do?'

'Oh, nothing. The extraction will expire on its own.' He picked up the metal tray and returned it to the shelves. He smiled at her. 'I bet you feel amazing now,' he said.

He hadn't cleaned the tray. A dribble of the creature's excretions leaked down the metal. She wanted to put her finger in the liquid, bring it to her lips.

The doctor approached her. He linked his arm with hers. 'You might not realise it immediately,' he said, leading her out through reception. 'But you will. This has been a monumental success.'

He beamed at her. He clasped her shoulder, then gently pushed her through the building entrance and out into the world.

The outside light was milky, thickly bright. She blinked into it, dazed. Across the street, the crowds swelled, broke apart, joined again. In between its ebbing, she spotted drops of maroon on the ground.

She crossed the road to follow the trail but found herself swallowed by the rhythm of the surrounding bodies. She tried to retrace her steps, scanning the pavement: waves of brogues, Chelsea boots. A child with a balloon, a pigeon with one eye. As she watched, the child let go of his balloon. It blew up into the sky, rising and rising until it flew far from sight.

The child turned to her, eyes filling with water. He opened his mouth wide, as if he was going to start screaming, but not a single sound emerged.

※

Susan kept making eye contact with her from across the room. When Catherine caught her, she would quickly turn her face to the computer, or out the window, or start chewing on her pen. She would then look back, lips twisting down.

Catherine smiled at her, and Susan's lips spasmed.

Everyone else avoided her eyes. She wondered if she was imagining the stiffness of their bodies as they walked past her desk, their heads kept down. When she stood to go to the breakroom, she saw several people flinch.

She drank a cup of coffee. She drank another, slower. While she was making her third, Susan came in. She lingered in the doorway. She clutched the handle so tightly that her knuckles turned white.

'Is something wrong?' she said.

'What?'

'You seem, I don't know, are you sick again?' Susan crossed into the room then blanched. She backed up against the wall, folding her arms.

'What makes you say that?'

She squinted, looking a little confused. 'I really don't know,' she said. She took a step forward and stopped. She shuddered.

'What's your relationship like with your mother, Susan?' Catherine drank the rest of her coffee. It was scalding, but the sensation seemed comfortably muted.

'Wonderful. Why?'

There was a smear of red on the wall behind Susan's head. It looked like a handprint.

'Yeah, me too,' Catherine said. 'I have really good parents. My childhood was beautiful.'

Susan went back to her desk. She poured antibacterial gel into her hands, rubbed them together vigorously.

Catherine knocked on Rob's door. He opened it without looking at her, typing something on his phone. He motioned for her to come in.

She came in, closing the door. 'Will you please have sex with me?'

He continued typing. 'We're at work. Don't be inappropriate.'

She started taking off her clothes. She lay down on the floor. The rough fibre of the carpet scratched the skin behind her knees.

Rob looked down at her and grimaced. 'Okay, but turn the other way.'

He put his phone on the ground beside her. He grabbed her hips and lined them up with his. She felt him lower his trousers, the metal buckle of his belt. The window of his office showed a grey sky, high-rise buildings. A dark liquid dripped down the glass pane. She thought she saw something moving just over the edge of the glass, but it flitted away. A blip of almost red, and then gone.

When he pushed into her, she reached over and took his phone. It was open on a text thread with his partner. She pressed the video call button and put the phone on the floor.

He pushed his forehead into her shoulder. He humped into her jaggedly, his breath irregular in her ear. She liked his open palm, held at a crooked angle on the floor. It looked soft.

'You're pathetic,' he moaned, getting quicker. 'You're so pathetic.'

He had security escort her out. His partner arrived as Catherine was removed from the office, her eyes red. 'There's something very wrong with you,' she sobbed, face puffy from tears.

Susan raised her head for a second when she went past, then lowered it.

On the pavement outside the office there was a pair of maroon footprints. She stepped on them; they were the same size as her own. She began to walk home.

Along the way, she stopped by the dog shelter. She tried to adopt the greyhound and was refused due to her lack of employment. The shelter warden left her alone in the room to euthanize a cat.

Catherine opened the cage that held the greyhound. She tried to coax him out, pulling gently at his collar. He licked her hands and retreated to the back of his cage. His expression was unspeakable.

She left the cage open. She left all the cages open. The shelter warden chased her from the building, a flurry of paws and tails and wings flooding past.

Catherine looked backwards as she ran. The shelter warden, the escapees. In the doorway of the shelter, a figure stood watching them. She couldn't make out its features but could see the dripping pool of maroon at its feet. The warden slowed, looking back too.

The figure stepped forward. It raised a hand and waved at her. It looked like it might be smiling.

Catherine raised her arm in return. She began to laugh. They waved at each other, smiling. Laughing, laughing.

NOTES ON PERFORMANCE

(Do you want me to tell you how it feels? Do you want me to tell you it hurts?

I could. I could tell you about how a knife goes through skin, and then sinew, and then bone. I could tell you about how a cut isn't always clean and how it's often a tear, rather than a slice. I could sketch you a diagram. We could get a spider and pull its legs off. I could tell you about pain.

I could tell you about things that are slick and warm and red, things that are hidden and whispered and wet. I could tell you about the worst thing that has ever happened to a person. I could make you blush blood bright.

Would you like me to tell you I enjoy it? Would you enjoy that more? Would you like me to tell you that you are a good person? Would you like me to tell you that it's going to be okay?

Would you like me to tell you a secret?)

'Have you ever been on film?' the director asked her. He sat behind a desk opposite the set, his assistant in the seat next to him.

Claire shook her head.

He stared at her, and then he repeated the question, enunciating each word slowly. His assistant laughed and then covered her mouth with her hand.

'No,' Claire said. The summer air was clogged with sawdust and pollen, making her voice croak.

'How old are you?' he asked.

'Eighteen.'

The director and the assistant exchanged a look. She wrote something down on her clipboard.

'Do you have previous experience?' the assistant asked.

'Not a lot, but I have some.' Claire went to fold her arms; the director caught the movement and his eyes narrowed. She froze midmotion, her arms hovering in the air.

'And "some" is?'

'I was part of the chorus for our parish's production of the Passion. I played a mourner. And I was an elf in Santa's grotto last December.'

The assistant smiled widely. She didn't write anything down. The director pulled up his sleeves and leaned forward on the desk, clasping his hands together. They were large and tanned, thick fingers sprinkled with dark hair around the knuckles. 'Do a spin,' he said. 'Make it slow.'

She spun, concentrating on keeping her head up. The director looked her up and down, lingering on her feet and neck. 'Pull your hair. Hard.'

She pulled sharply down on a fistful of curls, and her eyes watered. Through the blur, she saw the director nodding, rubbing his chin. He seemed thoughtful. 'Have you ever died before?' he asked.

'No.'

'I think you'd be good at it. You've got the look.' He turned to the assistant. 'Will you get the knife?' he asked. She raised an eyebrow and then reached below the desk, taking out a meat cleaver. The assistant brought it up to the set, holding it out to her.

'I actually wanted to audition for Lisa,' Claire said. 'I prepared the monologue.'

The director tutted. 'You're not going to be a final girl.'

'It's the eyes,' the assistant said.

'Yes!' the director said, clapping his hands together. 'Or the mouth. Something, yeah, it is, isn't it?'

'Cheap.'

'Yes!'

The assistant pushed the cleaver into her hand. She clenched her fingers around the handle, testing its weight. The metal was cool in her palm.

'Good, isn't it?' the director said.

She nodded, because it *was* good. The heft of it in her hand, heavy as slumber. It was very good.

The director slapped the desk and beckoned with a finger. She went to him. He reached across and took her wrist, placing her hand flat on the wooden surface. His hands were powdered with talcum. 'Just the pinkie,' he said. 'We just need to see if you'll be able to handle the role.'

She nodded and held the cleaver above her pinkie.

(Are you watching?)

The director kept his eyes on her face.

(Do you know what's about to happen?)

He briefly stroked his finger against her wrist, just a little.

(Are you excited?)

She brought the cleaver down, fast and hard. His mouth parted in a flicker of tongue and tooth as the knife went through. She thought it looked like a smile.

(What exactly do you want to see here?

You could go to a butcher. You could watch a bald, red-faced man cut a hunk of veal into thick, raw pieces. You are allowed to look at the pink juice that will run onto the white surface of the chopping board. No one will stop you watching.

If you want to see it live, you could go to a farm. If you need the smell. Or if you're tactile, maybe they will let you put a hand on the calf while they're doing it. They will let you feel the spasm of its muscles while it kicks out, the beat of its pulse thumping in a panicked rhythm under your palm, and then eventually the way the meat will cool and fall still.

I'm not going to judge you. I'm watching too.

Use your words. You don't have to be shy. Tell me what exactly you would like to see. Tell me why, exactly, you need to see it.)

The assistant reached below the desk again, pulling a plastic container from her handbag. She opened and shook it; a spattering of breadcrumbs fell out. She picked up the severed pinkie and dropped it in the container. She pushed the container into Claire's left hand. 'We'll be in touch, to let you know,' she said. She passed her the lid. The director was on his phone, scrolling through Twitter. He didn't look at Claire.

Her pinkie wiggled in the container, jerking against the side like a trapped animal. It left a faint red snail trail in its wake. The container smelled strongly of both copper and garlic salami. She put the lid on it and left.

On the bus home, the child in the aisle next to hers leaned over, peering into the container. His face was covered in something neon blue and crusted. 'Whoa,' he said. His breath was sickly sweet, like candy floss. He poked the top. The pinkie reared back, as if to strike.

His mother pulled him away. She looked down at the container and then at the neckline of Claire's blouse. Her mouth pinched to a prune. She shook her head and pulled the boy closer to her.

The pinkie began to thrash inside the box, arching back and forth in gushing sprays of glossy cherry. A man with grey hair standing near the window caught her eye. He looked between her and the box. He rubbed his thigh slowly and then winked.

She slid the container under her top, feeling the warm, jerking movement of the lid on her stomach.

At home, she sat down and put the container on the kitchen table. She opened it and picked the pinkie up. She expected it to thrash or scurry away, but it stilled its movement once it was out of the container and back in her hands. It leaned against her palm, nuzzling into the heart line. The skin of its underside was sticky with gore but tender to the touch.

The silence of the flat told her it was empty. She was glad. Her roommate was a nice, quiet student who did not make eye contact and tiptoed to the bathroom in clean, pastel socks. She never spoke but left wrapped baked goods out for Claire, the sticky notes on the cellophane telling her to have a lovely day. Claire didn't know how she would have explained her actions to a girl like that.

When she went to the bedroom, she saw that she had voicemail messages on her phone. She thought about what they might say. She deleted them without listening.

She dropped the pinkie on the bed and let it cosy into the blankets. She took the needle and thread from the drawers. She knew she should use antiseptic, but she had none and doubted her roommate would either.

Her phone pinged—an email. She opened it and found that she'd been given the role of Dead Girl #1.

Beside her, the pinkie rubbed against her thigh. She picked it up, placed it on the stub, and began to sew it back on, one black stitch at a time. The pinkie was docile and calm while she did this; it seemed glad to be home.

(You might be curious about what this part feels like. Is the act of reconciliation a beautiful moment? Would you weep if you too were a thing made of absences, suddenly to find yourself whole again?

If you have never sat in your bedroom, examining the parts of yourself that you have willingly cut off, you might never know. If you have never put parts of yourself back together while alone, one stitch at a time, then you might not ever understand.

It's okay if you're jealous. It's okay to want to be included.

As an exercise: to begin to understand something that is similar to this feeling, call your mother.

Tell her you are going away and will not return before she is dead. Tell her that you do not love her, that you never loved her. Tell her in explicit detail about the things you find physically repulsive in her (her dry, calloused fingertips, the caesar-

ean scar across her deflated stomach, the long, pointed nose that she later gave to you) and then the things in her that you find emotionally disappointing (her dull cowardice, her mindless passivity, her childlike fear of anyone who wasn't you).

She will apologise; hang up mid-apology. Block her number, delete your Facebook. Get a new number. Move to a new house, move to a new country—do not give her your address. When friends reach out to you on her behalf, block them too. Start a new job and tell your coworkers that your mother died in a fire.

After a while, return home abruptly without warning. When she answers the door, she will be quiet but physically affectionate. She will keep trying to hold you. She will make tea with too many sugars and turn on the heating and let the dog sit on the good leather couch.

She will sit you on the couch and turn on the television. She will ask you what you want to watch. She won't mention the way you sliced her off. Begin to sew the disparate parts together. Let her hold you, if you can stand it; it will warm you like a patch of sunlight on a phantom limb.

How did that feel? Do you want to do it again?)

She went to rehearsals the next day and didn't receive her script from the stagehand until midmorning. The stagehand had a quiet voice and a tremor in his hands; when he handed her the script, the words trembled on the page like newborn babes.

He said something under his breath. She had to lean in to hear him, close enough that she could see a patch of razor burn next to his mouth acne.

'—not many lines,' he murmured, looking down at the page. The sentences shook, blurring to a frenzy. 'Very sorry.'

'No, no, it's fine!'

He nodded to the floor, back hunched. She could see the knots of his spine through his thin T-shirt. 'Really, fine!' she said again. She took the script and patted his elbow; he froze and then raised his gaze to her chin.

The director walked up and slapped the stagehand on the back. The stagehand jerked away from the touch. He closed his eyes and took short, sharp breaths. His knuckles were white, clutching the bottom of his T-shirt.

'Why isn't she with hair and makeup?' the director asked.

She was taken to a small, white room. There were sharp chemicals in the air that made her think of swimming pools.

The stylists wore face masks and had brightly dyed hair set in elaborate updos. They didn't say much to her but talked to each other as they sat her in a swivel chair. Their chatter was lilting and musical, like so many songbirds in a flurry around her.

'How old are you?' one asked. Her pink hair floated in the air above her, twisting in spiralling dances.

'Eighteen.'

'We need to go younger.' One of the pink coils slithered down her neck, wrapping itself around her throat.

They started with the eyes. They tightened the skin around the sides, pinching it up with an intricate wrench-like object. The twisting feeling of the stretching skin was both sore and satisfying, like brushing out knots in tangled hair. They fixed the taut skin in place behind her temples with tacky, clear glue.

They massaged the sockets of her eyes and applied an ointment that made the bone soften, and then pulled at the hole with careful, gentle movements, widening her gaze. Their fingers were cold and soothing on her face as they made the facial adjustments; she thought they might be wearing aloe vera hand cream.

They held up a mirror to let her see. 'I look frightened,' she said.

'Don't worry, it's not very permanent,' one of them said.

After that, they took out a needle, which was marked as seal blubber, and inserted it in her face. Her cheeks were fattened until she felt them bulging out in puppy plumpness and rouged and freckled with the airbrushing tool.

The stylists looked her up and down.

'The body,' one said. She couldn't tell which one spoke because of the face masks, but they all nodded together in agreement.

'Take two, three ribs?'

'Please, and shorten the femur. We want a total body length of sixty-one inches maximum.'

'B-cup?'

'No, don't decrease size, but do increase the areola saturation by two shades.'

Before they put her to sleep for the longer surgeries, they gave her a glass of water with lemon and turned on the radio. One of them hummed along to the melody while injecting her and ran fingers through Claire's hair.

When she woke, she was in a hospital gown and the director was looking down at her. She went to sit up, and he put his hand on her leg.

'Don't move,' he said. She didn't move.

He moved his hand down to her feet. 'They're smaller,' he said. He ran his hand up her leg, over her hip, and then held her jaw. He pinched her cheek hard, and she winced. He nodded, looking pleased. 'Good,' he said.

(**Do you want to know which of them I lose my virginity to? Would you like to see?**

Sorry, trick question. Final girls are virgins. Final girls have something to lose, and I am not a final girl. If I was, I could let you watch. We could film it and press rewind and watch it together, if you liked.

We could see if it was the director. That would be interesting for a little while, and then it wouldn't be. Dead girls do not have high enough stakes for this. It is unsurprising when he is sadistic and selfish and leaves me raw and open. It is predictable that he would go back to his wife or fall in love with the blonde lead, Lisa, with her petite toddler tits and gentle gaze, and buy her large bouquets of laughing sunflowers while I watch from the back of the room, feeling my neck for bruises.

It could be the stagehand, with his protruding rib cage and apologetic touch. Would you like to see him get the girl? Doesn't he deserve it?

I can let you peep through the hole in his bedroom wall where he takes me one day after rehearsals. You can watch his shaking hand stutter under my thong and scratch my labia painfully when the jagged edge of his uncut nail catches on the lip. We could pause the scene, if this upsets you. If it arouses you, we can come back to it.

It's only pretend. I have never been a virgin. But what would you like to see?)

For the death scene, she wore a pleated skirt and a small gold crucifix that fell down into the dip of the half-buttoned shirt.

'Am I a schoolgirl? What age am I?' she asked the pink-haired stylist as she plaited her hair. The stylist shrugged.

She looked down at the script. The stagehand had told her she didn't have many lines, but she didn't have any lines. She didn't even have a name. She was going to kiss an unnamed father while babysitting his infant, and then they were both going to be murdered. He was going to be wearing a suit and would be stabbed in the chest. She would be topless and show partial nipple while being asphyxiated over the course of exactly two and a half minutes. Her body was going to then be brutalised with a machete and scattered throughout the house. The stylist stepped back and surveyed her. 'You're perfect for the part,' she said.

'Thank you,' Claire said. 'That's very nice of you.'

She turned a page in the script, and the stylist grabbed her hand. She lifted Claire's pinkie finger.

'This isn't tidy enough,' she said, picking at the stitches.

'I'd never done it before.'

The stylist frowned and got the airbrushing tool and cleaned up the mistakes in her stitches, then she led Claire out to the set. The director was in his chair, the assistant beside him.

The unnamed father walked up to Claire, looking at her chest. 'So!' he said. 'God, ha!' He rubbed his hands together.

'Yeah!' she said. 'Ha!'

The killer walked up to the director. He was already in costume, the large horse mask covering his head. He and the director hugged tightly. The director laughed at something the killer said and then kissed him on his plastic snout and slapped him on the back. The director looked from him to Claire and grinned. 'Okay,' he said. 'Let's begin.'

They all got into place. She sat beside the father and put her hands on his shoulders. She looked at his face and tried to decide if he was handsome. His jaw was weaker than the director's, and he had bloodshot eyes.

The director came over to them. He leaned forward and undid a button on her shirt and pulled a few strands of hair loose from her plaits. He pulled one of the plaits hard. She tried to repress the wince, but he nodded anyway and smiled. 'Exactly, yeah, you're a pro,' he said. His aftershave was heavy with peppercorn and made her feel lightheaded.

He returned to his seat. From the corner of her eye she could see the killer just off set, the knife in his hand. The director winked at him and the killer gave him a thumbs-up.

'Okay, action,' the director said. They began.

(**Are you a fan of hentai? Because of censorship laws, genitals and pubic hair are often blurred out during male–female intercourse. Skinny, pale cartoon girls with their eyes wide and legs spread, little clouds of pixelated dots hovering over their pelvises. You would think this would make it less erotic. You would think hiding something would dull the effect. But it's more like costumed monsters in black-and-white films, the ones we never fully see. We are allowed glimpses of claw, tooth,** and wings, and are denied the full sight. Because of this, we imagine a monster so much worse.)

The killer looked at her.

(One time, a final girl was sick and couldn't make rehearsal, and the director asked me to read her part.

There were many lines. I spoke quietly. My voice frightened me, the feel of it in my throat. It was rough and unpredictable; I rarely used my mouth for speech on set. The male lead gnashed his bleached teeth when I was asked to repeat myself, ran a hand across his forehead. The flesh of his face was supple, dewed tender with coconut oil.

The director came over, stood in front of me. He placed his hands on my elbows, bending slightly to look up into my gaze. His eyes were smiling. He leaned close, murmuring into my ear. His breath damp, latte-sweet.

We both know how good you could be.

It was wonderful to say 'stop,' and for something to stop. It was wonderful to scream, and for the sound to be heard. It was wonderful to run, and to get away. It was wonderful to be a different kind of girl. I spoke loudly, and I spoke clearly. I was gentle, and brave, and kind. I was good, and no one hurt me. I did not have to die.

The director took me to dinner after the rehearsal. He helped me out of my coat, held open doors. The waiter wouldn't look me in the eye but pulled out my chair, bowing, blushing. We had steaming plates of prawn linguini, thin-stemmed glasses of hissing cava. The bubbles tickled my lips, laughter fizzing out of my mouth. I avoided my reflection in the silverware; a different face might be there.

He asked me to tell him something secret, something that no one else knew.

I didn't say: *I miss my mother so much, and I can no longer stand to look her in the eye. I haven't been held in a very long time.*

I didn't say: *I don't have many friends because I am jealous of other women and can only view men through a sexual lens.*

I didn't say: *On dates with the stagehand, I pretend not to know film directors because I like to make him like me. It feels better than liking him. Once, he asked me if I had ever heard of Hitchcock. I said yes and he looked sad, and then he looked bored. Since then, if he asks me if I have heard of a director, I say no, and he puffs up with pride like a comfortable pigeon while telling me about their oeuvre. My disgust for him in these moments is outweighed by the power of knowing I have made him feel needed and knowledgeable and masculine. My contempt and my satisfaction mix to a sickly, electric thrill in my stomach. After this rush, I feel ungrounded and dizzy, a kite without tether. I kiss him and do my best to imagine the texture of my own tongue.*

I didn't say: *I asked the stagehand if he would like to hit me during sex. He was confused and upset by the question. He tried to hit me but kept hesitating and I said, 'Just do it, just do it, you fucking pussy,' and I felt him soften while inside of me. We stopped and he began to cry and I got up and held him from behind, rubbing his sides and arms. A different time, he asked if he could pretend to be the director while we did it. He punched me without asking and seemed to find it much more enjoyable. After the act was done, I would feel woozy with pleasure while thinking about how much he had enjoyed himself.*

I didn't say: *I am not sure if I enjoy being hurt or not. I really don't know.*

I didn't tell him any of that. This is just for you.)

The director didn't bother calling 'cut' on the scene when it finished. He just stood, stretching his neck from side to side until it cracked. He picked up his coffee. 'Forty minutes,' he said to the room at large before walking out the fire exit.

The crew began to exit the set. Sandwiches and cigarette packets were scooped out of duffel bags, nervous laughter rising through the room like a layer of smoke, warm and overwhelming. After the room emptied, only she and the father remained. Very slowly, he moved his hands towards his chest wound, feeling around the edge of the knife. He tugged it out bit by bit, groaning at the slow pull. He dropped the knife down on the couch next to him when it was free. It dripped onto the leather of the couch, the blood thickening as it cooled. He got up with a grunt and looked around him. He spotted her in the corner. 'See you after lunch!' he said with a wave, and left the set.

Claire tried to wave back, but her arm was at the other side of the room, jammed under the TV unit. It gave a feeble little jerk, but there wasn't enough space for it to wave.

She focused her attention on the arm, watching it moving out from the unit one inch at a time. It used its fingers to pull itself along. The arm pressed its fingertips into the ground and dragged the weight of itself forward; Claire winced at the squeaking sound it made as the skin of the wrist got caught on the polished, wooden floor.

The arm tugged its way across the set until it got to her. The hand reached out to clutch at her face, then the damp, sticky stump of her neck. She leaned her face into the hand, letting it hold her in its palm. It stroked her cheek with a finger in a soothing, gentle rhythm.

She tried to glance around the room, looking for other parts of herself. She saw a leg, a lung, teeth and toes and several ribs scattered along the bookshelves like splatterings of confetti.

The pieces that could move came towards her, wriggling across the quiet set. She sent her arm out after the bits that couldn't move, pulling them across the room until they were all huddled in a pile in front of her.

She looked at herself. She was surprised by how much of her there was. She'd thought the pile would be smaller, but all her raw, fragile fragments made a large sum. She tried to make sense of the broken pieces, but all she could see was so much meat.

She heard someone whistling. She glanced up and saw the director leaning down beside his chair. He looked up at her. 'Forgot my phone.' He held it up in the air. On the lock screen, there was a picture of the director and a little boy. The director leaned towards the boy in the picture, pressing a smiling kiss against his cheek. The boy was beaming and holding a fistful of dandelions, shoving them towards the camera with glee.

He walked over to her. He smiled. 'You did really good today, Claire,' he said. 'I'm really proud of you.'

'Really?'

'Really. I think you're a very talented girl.'

Claire felt her cheeks redden. She could see her heart in the pile of organs, pumping in and out in a fast rhythm. *Thank you*, she tried to say, but a giggle escaped instead.

The director slid the phone into his pocket. 'When the crew comes back, they can help you sew up, if you need.' He paused and frowned slightly. 'In future, bring your own sewing equipment to do it yourself. More professional,' he said, and winked. He walked back towards the exit. He stopped at the door.

'Claire?'

'Yes?'

'I hope we work together again,' he said, and left.

(Contrary to popular belief, the first time isn't as important as you might think. There's so much more to come.

Don't worry about damage. My body is stronger than yours. It can allow itself to be broken over and over. I am acquainted with leaking, wounding. I know very well how to bleed.

Do you want to break something? Would you like to show me how strong you are?

The first time was exactly whatever you imagined. It was a blur of skin and limbs and dripping holes. If you want, it could have been very painful. Or not at all.

We can have many times together. I am seventeen and a babysitter. I am a cheerleader. I am a cheating spouse. I am a stepdaughter. I am a tourist on holiday and a drunk girl in a nightclub and a stripper in glitter and a woman walking home alone at night and an unloving mother and a girl who didn't text you back and your ex-girlfriend and the girl who fucked your ex-girlfriend and the wife that won't let a kind man see his kids and a corpse that didn't get a name or a head

but wore pretty silver nail polish on her toes in flip-flops and was dismembered part by part and the parts were burned and thrown in the sea and then not mentioned again for the rest of the movie.

There will be so many more times. The director loves me.)

EGGSHELLS

She felt her stomach cramp as the egg began to move downwards.

Sunrise leaked through the curtains, shadows blushing. Beside her, Luke's sleep-sour breath, tickling her cheek. She took the lube out of the side desk. She poured a cool, clear dollop on her palm, pulled down her underwear, and held her labia apart. The folds were dry and sensitive, and when she began to massage the lube in, she felt the tender skin recoil at the cold shock.

'Do you want me to help?' Luke said, voice small. His erection pressed against her thigh.

'No.' She tried to press her fingers in deeper, but it was sore, the stiff muscle tensing as the cramps grew.

'What if it cracks again?'

'Please go back to sleep.'

'You woke me. I'm just trying to help.'

'I don't need help.' She removed her fingers from her hole, wiping them on the blanket.

The egg was coming; she grimaced at the building pressure. She pushed hard, clenching her fists. Her muscles spasmed, and then the egg was moving through her, slipping smoothly down the vaginal walls. The egg was full and firm but the stretch mostly painless.

'Don't forget to catch it,' Luke said. Lisa rolled her eyes and moved her hand just below her opening. A moment later, the egg popped out with a small squelch, dropping into her palm.

The egg was a light tan, specked with brown freckles. It glistened in the early morning light, drooling with lube. The greased shell felt warm as blood.

'It's getting on the blanket,' Luke said. She stood and placed the egg in the incubation box opposite the bed.

'Did you do your positive associations last night?' he asked.

She thought about not answering. 'You should go,' she said.

She heard his silence, then rustling sheets. She tapped the egg with her finger. His lips on her shoulder. Brief, dry. 'I'll text you,' he said.

She showered and dressed. After, she checked the incubation box, removing the lid.

The shell lay in splinters. In the corner of the transparent box, a fish thrashed, bashing its tail against the side. It was pink and had grown larger than the egg it had hatched from. When it saw her looking, it stilled. It lifted its neck and smiled, its mouth filled with large, square teeth.

'You piece of shit,' it said. Its breath smelled of cloves.

She hummed and stooped, checking for abnormalities. Instead of scales, a layer of skin, rosy as a newborn. One eye missing, three extra fins on its belly. She grabbed her phone and input the info into her cycle app. She put the lid back on and left for her shift at the restaurant.

She came home late. The box was spattered with yolk. The fish lay unmoving. She sponged the box clean, then disposed of the hatchling and shell, dropping them into the kitchen compost bin. She rinsed the dirtied sponge under the sink, watching the water run gold.

She opened Luke's texts and waited seventy minutes to reply. He arrived within ten minutes, a loaf of bread cradled in the crook of his arm, rocking it back and forth.

'I made it myself,' he said, beaming.

She took the bread and put it on the counter. 'I'm sure you did,' she said.

She had him get on his knees and eat her out at the kitchen table. She yanked at the roots of his hair and called him a good boy while he pulled himself off, let him cry against her leg after he came in his pants. He pressed his forehead into her knee, snot-nosed and panting. Eventually, he stood.

'I should go.' His eyes were red, his mouth swollen. He wiped his nose with the back of his hand and stared at a spot on the floor.

'Cool!' she said. She walked him to the door.

Before she went to sleep that night, she found a podcast for guided associations. She pressed play and closed her eyes.

'Imagine a small, white cat,' the guide whispered. 'Imagine its fur on your skin. It is good, and clean, and it is yours. You are good, and clean, and your body is yours. You are in control. Imagine the cat. The cat is beautiful. You are capable of beautiful things.'

❧

The cat that emerged from the egg on Tuesday morning didn't have eyes. There were no sockets for eyes to grow in, just a furry flat plane on the top half of its face. It made a whining noise when she opened the lid. Lisa reached down to stroke it. The fur was matted and infested with lice. It purred when she stroked it, but then it let out a low, masculine moan. She withdrew her hand, and the cat chuckled. 'Luke is as good as it gets,' it said.

She forgot to listen to the podcast that night but did watch *The Phantom of the Opera* (2004). On Wednesday morning, the daily egg cracked and hundreds of flies emerged, swarming the box. They were lavender and collectively buzzed out the melody of 'Angel of Music.'

She clapped when they finished. All at once their wings fell off and they dropped out of the air. One of the flies crawled to the glass and shook a tiny fist at her.

'Your mam feels alone all the time,' the fly said. 'She is afraid to go to shops because of large crowds. Her heating broke and she is very cold and you told her you'd get someone to fix it but you didn't. Her tits sag to her belly button and their heavy weight hurts her back and sometimes when she looks in the mirror she starts crying. You never call. She thinks about how you never call. She thinks about it all the time.'

She called Mam that evening. Mam told her about Pat from next door who had fixed her heating and about every member of the parish who had recently died. Lisa half listened, thinking about how she was going to tell Mam she loved her.

'Are you seeing anyone?' Mam asked, interrupting the thought.

'Why?'

'Pat's single.'

'All right?'

'I'm only saying.' She cleared her throat, phlegmy and harsh. 'How are your eggs?'

'You can't ask people that.'

'So I'm not allowed to worry. Lovely.'

'Mam.'

'Are you even doing your associations?'

'Not your business, is it?'

'It'll be your own fault, if there're abnormalities. I hope you have some cop on. At your big age.'

Mam began to cough. Her lungs sounded sticky, tobacco-syrup thick. She waited for Mam to catch her breath.

The coughing didn't stop. It grew a little quieter, like Mam had moved away from the phone. She listened for a minute, and then she hung up.

She texted Luke asking him to come over. For twenty minutes the icon showed her that Luke was typing. She turned off her phone and went to bed.

⚘

She was late for work the next morning and had to lay the egg as quickly as she could, straining her muscles. She tried to piss after it was in the box. She noticed drops of blood in the bowl; it had been a while since she had ripped anything.

She returned to her bedroom. Inside the box sat a baby.

Lisa touched her stomach. 'I'm not pregnant,' she said.

'No, I'm not a real baby. Just a hatchling, don't worry!' he said. He had a crisp, rich accent, like a presenter on the news.

'Oh, that's good.' Lisa sat down on the bed, looking at the box.

The baby smiled at her. He tried to sit up, but his head lolled to the side, unable to hold its weight.

'Can I come out?' he asked.

'I don't think I'm meant to. My mam told me letting hatchlings out gives you irregular cycles.'

'You're probably infertile. And you'd be a terrible mother. You're a bad person. You are deeply selfish and fundamentally lacking in the generosity and depth of character needed to love another. So, you may as well.' The baby winked.

She took him out. He was a beautiful baby, blemish-free, but his skin was sticky with yolk and left a slimy layer on her fingers.

She lay back down in bed, holding him in her arms. 'I don't even like children,' she said. The baby hummed and nuzzled into her chest. His skin left a yellow stain on the white of her pyjama top.

'That's not really the point, though, is it?'

'No,' she said.

She realised the baby's movements were growing slower. He cocked a fair eyebrow at her. 'Want to put me back in the box?'

She shook her head. He gurgled and grabbed at her hand, beaming. She let him clutch her finger. Eventually, his grip relaxed.

She lay there for longer than she should have, then went to work, leaving the hatchling in the bed.

For the first hour, she felt fine. In the second she felt light-headed, the warm smoke and metallic screeching of the kitchen leaving her dazed. Her stomach began to cramp while she carried two plates across the floor, heading towards two men in the back booth. She took a breath as the pain hit her abdomen. She closed her eyes, focusing on her breathing, and then continued walking. She reached the booth and smiled at the pair.

'Smoked salmon?' she said. One of the men nodded, unsmiling. As she lowered the plates, the pain shifted downwards. It snaked through her belly, down along her pelvis. A heavy pressure was building in her groin.

Her eyes snapped open as she realised what was happening. She stood up, dropping the plates. The hollandaise sauce spilled over the men. They leapt up as she took a step back, hoping to get to the toilets before it happened. Then, she felt something crack.

She froze. She looked down at her crotch. The grey of her trousers had darkened. In the wet patch, yolk seeped through, gold globs oozing down her inner thigh.

'Lisa,' someone whispered.

Someone laughed and someone else made a hushing sound. Someone sighed; it sounded like her mother.

Her manager called her into the storeroom for a talk. 'This is very inappropriate,' he said. 'I mean, in public. Really, Lisa.'

'I didn't mean to. I already had one this morning.'

'Oh. Is this, uh . . . ' he said. He fiddled with the plastic wrapping of a unit of saltshakers, adjusting the box. 'Unusual? For you?'

'Why?'

'If you're feeling unwell, management should know. We're here to support the mental health of our employees. Positive mind, positive eggs, all that.'

She stared at him. He continued to adjust the box. It squeaked as he slid it back and forth.

'Fantastic,' she said. 'I'm fantastic.'

She turned to leave and felt the crunch of a piece of shell inside her as she moved.

❧

She finally opened Luke's texts. The word 'aftercare' was used, the word 'unfair,' the word 'selfish.' Then there were several apologies, a plea to come over, a picture of his erect cock. She sent a thumbs-up. She cleaned up the box and removed the hatchling from the bed. She held it for a moment, feeling its heft. She disposed of it in the kitchen and then washed her hands in the sink. The water was scalding; she blinked into the hot steam, watching red blossom on the skin of her wrists.

She stayed up all night watching YouTube compilations of positive eggs. Fat, large-eyed rabbits, quivering tails on rounded rumps as plump and downy as a fuzzy peach. More ambitious creations: sleeping unicorns the size of teacups, miniature dragons with flames that blew no hotter than a mellow summer breeze.

'It's all about focus,' one of the women said, holding the dragon on her palm. 'Self-control. Positivity. Not that hard!' She laughed as the dragon did a cartwheel around her fingers.

She didn't realise it was morning until she felt the cramp. She considered soiling herself. Instead, she took out the lube and began to prep. Pieces of shell from the last egg were still inside her. She picked them out gently. The yolk had dried on the folds of her vulva and smelled rich and sour.

When the egg was out and in the incubation box, she got a

makeup wipe from the bathroom. She wiped the yolk from her crotch and then came back to check the box.

The egg was split down the middle in two halves, unnaturally symmetrical, and the box was empty.

She lifted the egg, dipping a finger in. The shell was dry, fragile, and entirely clean of yolk. She pressed the halves against her cheek, feeling for warmth.

She placed the shell down on the blanket as gently as she could. She thought about calling someone, but she didn't know what she would say.

She got toilet paper from the bathroom and rolled it around the shell, layers and layers of white swaddling to keep it safe. She picked it up, clutching it loosely in one palm so as not to crush it.

She went down to her car and got in, placing the wrapped shell in the passenger seat. For a brief moment she thought about putting the seat belt around it, and then she started laughing at the ridiculous thought. Then she couldn't stop laughing and then she couldn't breathe and her chest hurt so badly that she thought she might just die. She drove to her mam's house, being careful to not go too quickly for fear of knocking the shell about.

She knocked on the door, but there was no answer. She pressed the doorbell for a few minutes before remembering it no longer worked and that she had said she would get someone to fix it. She looked through the front window. The light was off, and the shadows distorted the room; she couldn't recognise any of the faces in the framed photographs, and the furniture seemed menacing and wrong.

She sat down on the front step, placing the shell in her lap. She was glad she had wrapped it up before she left; the sun hadn't risen yet, and it was so cold out that she could see her breath.

She flexed her fingers to keep them warm. She wanted to tighten her hands and arms around the cushioned parcel, to seek a sliver of comfort or warmth. She kept her hands by her sides, tensing her muscles rigidly until they ached. She wasn't sure how to hold the eggshell without cracking it into pieces; even trying seemed a crime. She wrapped her arms around herself to keep them restrained. She leaned back into the door and pressed her cheek against the cold wood, listening for movement within.

The morning was dark around her. She stayed as still as she could, waiting for light to bloom.

THE TEST

'Are you a virgin?'

Niamh blinked at the doctor. She didn't look like any doctor Niamh had seen before. Her family's own physician, Bernadette Grant, had greying hair, crow's-feet, a quiet voice. Her hands were so kind, so clean when they checked for hurt with slow and careful movements.

The woman in front of her didn't look like Dr Grant. Dark, sleek feathers grew from her head, and the skin on her cheeks wriggled and stretched from time to time, as if there was something underneath. It reminded Niamh of the dead cat she had once found in her garden, the pouch of its belly squirming with maggots.

The room didn't look like a doctor's office either. The doctor sat in a tall throne chair, twirling a stethoscope in a circle as she looked down at Niamh. There was no other furniture in the room, apart from a small, wooden school desk. The desk didn't have a chair, so Niamh hovered behind it, half-crouched. The ground was covered in thick layers of dust, piling up to her ankles. Clouds of the powder rose whenever Niamh shifted; every movement made her choke, eyes watering. She left footprints wherever she stepped. 'What?' Niamh asked.

'Have you ever let a man enter you?'

Niamh froze. Jack Matthews had shoved it up her ass once without warning when they were dating. She'd bled on and off for a day and a half. She remembered looking at the red specks on the paper after she'd used the toilet. *What a waste*, she had thought.

'No. I'm saving myself.'

The doctor's eyes changed colours, from bright yellow to a glowing red. 'So you're inexperienced, then?'

The doctor wrote something down in her chart. Niamh leaned over—**PRUDE** was written in big, blocky letters. *Shit*, Niamh thought.

'No! I mean, I've done stuff. Just not everything.'

The doctor's eyes narrowed. Her talons gripped her pen tightly. 'What "stuff"? Be specific.'

'I've been fingered a couple of times. And I've performed oral?'

The doctor wrote the word **BORING** on her chart.

'I've been penetrated—ah, anal penetration?'

The doctor hooted, feathers shooting up. She grinned at Niamh, wiggled her eyebrows, and made a note in her chart. **SLUT** was written in even larger lettering than before.

Niamh was beginning to sweat. 'I didn't like it, though. I hated it,' she said. Her voice quivered. The doctor made a cooing noise and scratched her chin with her talon. Another note—**VANILLA**. She drew arrows connecting this word to the previous ones.

'Right, we'll take a urine sample to confirm my diagnosis, and then you can be off on your way,' she said. 'Library next.' She passed Niamh a urine cup.

'Here?' Niamh asked. The doctor nodded and made a hurrying motion with her talons.

Niamh turned, trying to shield herself with the desk, and tugged down her knickers. She thought of herself and Aoife pissing in bushes or behind trees after cans with Jack and his friends. She did her best to visualise a generous, leafy bush as she squeezed out a few drops, hands trembling. She placed the cup on the desk and turned around, unable to look at the doctor.

The door slammed behind Niamh as she exited the doctor's office, hitting the back of her head. Her skull hurt, and there was a little pee on her hands.

She looked down the dark corridor. The darkness seemed thicker than it should have been; if she threw something at it, something would bounce back. She wished Aoife were here. She wanted to keep walking, but she didn't know how to get to the library. She didn't know anything about the castle, or the fairy king. He hadn't needed a new wife in centuries.

'Hello?' she called. As if listening, the darkness suddenly shifted, swirling in sleek, smoky circles; it moved like an undertow. Niamh wondered if she was seeing things, but then the darkness slithered towards her, slipping between her ankles. It moved quickly upwards, cold on the skin of her thighs, and then her neck. She tried to back away, but it was seeping up her nose, crawling down her throat.

'Please,' she said, and it stopped. She felt it buzz, bulging in her throat, pressing against her uvula. She wondered if she would vomit, but then the darkness was leaking out, her airways freed.

She looked down; the darkness was glowing pink. It wasn't darkness anymore so much as a pillow of pink cloud that stretched down the corridor, giving off a faint light. It was humming, an old radio crackle; a song, growing louder by the second. Niamh knew that song, but it sounded off. Sad, strange synth; sickly sweet croon; dark, pleading bass. Something from a John Hughes movie, but all wrong. It was meant to be a love song, but love songs didn't sound like that.

The cotton-candy cloud glowed brighter, parting for her, showing her the way. It seemed cheery; she wondered if it liked when she begged. She walked on, letting it take the lead.

∞

The pink puff reached the big, dark door, and poofed out of being. Iron doorknobs shaped like gaping eyes; Niamh didn't want to touch them. She lifted her hand to knock on the door, but the eyes blinked, iron creaking. One eye winked at her; the door opened.

Large, long room, stone walls lined with bookshelves. Rows and rows of desks; a girl sitting at every desk, gazing at her. Everywhere, there were eyes, watching. 'You're late,' a voice whispered. Niamh whipped her head around, spinning in a circle, but no one was there.

'Take a seat and begin the exam.' The whisper was low, deep, more pulse than voice. It sent a ripple through the room; some of the books fell off the shelves. Niamh nodded to no one and walked to the first empty desk she found. Paper on desk, pot of ink, a white feathered quill. She sat, picking up the exam paper. At the top of the page, a single question: *How are you different to other girls?*

Niamh frowned. She dipped the quill in the ink; pink, again. The colour was beginning to make her feel sick. Earlier, pink was the colour of cotton candy; now, pink was the colour of meat bled dry. *I am different to other girls because*, she wrote, and stopped. Was she different? She began to make a possible list.

I am prettier than other girls.

That wasn't true. Jack told her she was pretty, but Evan Quilty had said to Jack that her nostrils made her look like a pig. So many girls in the room were pretty; Aoife had the plumpest lips Niamh had ever seen. Sometimes Niamh made herself look at the ground when Aoife smiled at her so she wouldn't stare at them. She crossed it out, wondering whereabouts Aoife was in the room.

~~*I am prettier than other girls.*~~
I am smarter than other girls.

Also not true. Niamh was good at history, but Aoife demolished her in science. Niamh loved listening to her talk about it, even if she didn't understand a word she said. She crossed it out.

~~*I am prettier than other girls.*~~
~~*I am smarter than other girls.*~~
I am funnier than other girls.

Niamh had once made Aoife laugh so hard that she pissed her pants a little in the middle of Tesco and had to borrow a pair of jeans from Niamh to wear home. Jack never really laughed at her jokes, though. She crossed it out.

She was beginning to feel crazed. She nibbled at the edge of the quill, bits of feather sticking between her teeth. She tried to peer into the paper of the girl next to her, but she was too far away.

~~*I am prettier than other girls.*~~

~~I am smarter than other girls.~~

~~I am funnier than other girls.~~

I give a great blow job, she wrote, hysteria rising.

Untrue. She'd tried to suck Jack off once and he'd thrusted too hard, hitting the back of her throat. She'd vomited all over both him and herself—he had dumped her shortly after.

She was getting giddy. She wanted to laugh and howl at the same time. She underlined the word *great*. She crossed it out.

~~I am prettier than other girls.~~

~~I am smarter than other girls.~~

~~I am funnier than other girls.~~

~~I give a great blow job~~

Fuck you, she wrote.

Niamh paused, hearing a roll of thunder. She raised her head; the walls of the room went up and up, the dusty stone growing green with mould and moss the higher the walls went, vines and thorns spilling out from the crumbling cracks miles above their heads. She didn't know where the walls of the room ended; they went up so high that she could see clouds forming far above their heads, grey and growling.

She felt something touch her cheek; the sky was raining pink petals. Millions of them were falling from the sky, heavy as a snowstorm. They quickly formed piles on the ground. Girls were getting up to play in the mounds, throwing petals into the air, flinging them at each other, winding them into their hair. They had forgotten about the test, and looked like they were having a wonderful time.

Niamh looked down at her sheet, covered in petals. She grasped a handful and pressed them to her face. For just a moment, she let herself close her eyes and thought of nothing but how very good they felt, like so many kisses gracing her cheek.

She dropped them, and the loss was enough to make her throat ache. She could hear the other girls laughing, squealing, sighing with pleasure as they rolled around in the luxurious piles, thoughtless in their easy joy.

All at once, Niamh felt very small.

She crossed out the entire paragraph, over and over, pressing the quill so hard that the page ripped.

I am prettier than other girls.
I am smarter than other girls.
I am funnier than other girls.
I give a great blow job
Fuck you.

*I give a **really** great blow job*, she wrote under the angry mess of ink. She threw her pen down on the desk and stood, went to join the others in the storm.

❧

Aoife met her on the way out of the exam. She frowned at the petals scattered on the floor, shaking her head. She reached over and brushed a few off Niamh's shoulders, her mouth pinching in distaste.

'What did you write?' she asked.

'That I give a great blow job.'

Aoife looked delighted. 'I knew you'd lie.'

'What did you write?'

'Didn't write anything.'

Niamh froze, turning to her friend. 'What?'

'I left it blank.'

Niamh thought of all her scratched-out words. She thought about Aoife's clear, cool sheet of indifference, the icy beauty of it, and decided she hated herself. She hated Aoife too, just a little.

'That's genius. Christ, you'll stand out a mile,' Niamh said.

Aoife frowned at her. 'Why would I want that?'

'What? Why wouldn't you?'

'Are you being thick? I hardly want to ride a rapist. Or marry one.'

Niamh halted and looked around her. A few girls on the corridor had gone quiet and were staring over at them. Niamh grabbed Aoife by the elbow and pulled her to the side, away from the crowd.

'Christ, Aoife. You can't say stuff like that.'

'Why not? What about all the girls that go missing when he's around? The ones that are too young or too poor. He comes to town, and they disappear, and no one talks about it.'

Niamh rubbed her arms and checked behind Aoife to see if anyone was listening. She stepped forward so she could lower her voice. 'You can't make accusations like that.'

Aoife stared at her. She shook her head. 'You're a coward,' she said.

A loud, deep, booming sound began to ring out above their heads. The two girls looked up. A large grandfather clock flew over them on a pair of beating wings, tolling the time. The face of the clock looked like human skin, but the hands appeared to be wood. The hybridisation looked painful. Two watery eyes looked down at the girls from above the handles, bloodshot and wide and filled with tears; it looked afraid. It flew past them and continued its job despite its obvious terror.

Aoife looked back at Niamh. 'I hate this,' she said.

Niamh nodded. 'Yeah,' she said. She tried to smile, and Aoife looked like she was trying to smile back.

'Where to next?'

Aoife's smile stuttered. 'Beauty contest in the main hall.'

⁓

The girls followed the crowd to the hall, hundreds of girls trailing through the corridor to the destination.

The hall looked newer than the library, colder and cleaner. The room was sleek black marble from floor to ceiling, windowless slabs dotted with neon bulbs, their light faint and flickering. Niamh could see her reflection in the oiled shine of the walls: a smudge of open mouth, a blur of yellow hair.

Her reflection waved at her, spun in a circle, and ran away into the darkness—Niamh had not moved an inch.

The room was crowded with girls preparing in front of vanity mirrors, in various stages of undress, sitting in ball gowns, black slips, Brazilian underwear, carefully applying lip liner. An overwhelming smell hung over the room: burnt marshmallow, peony perfume, summer-damp thongs. Niamh thought it smelled a bit like the colour pink.

They grabbed an empty vanity to share. Niamh found some foundation close to her shade on a shelf below and began to slap it on. Aoife took out her phone and scrolled through Twitter.

'Aren't you going to get ready?' Niamh asked.

'Nope.'

Niamh felt a flicker of something like annoyance, but closer to envy. She stared at her shiny, slightly too-orange face in the mirror. She rushed through her makeup, slathering on mascara and gloss. She felt greasy and ugly and needy and pathetic. She wanted to go home and be alone and never be looked at by another human again.

She looked around the room. Glamorous faces, silk gowns, dipping necklines. Then she saw other things.

Girls in gimp suits. Girls in rope, trussed like raw chicken. Girls supergluing real cat tails to their asses, mashing the bloody stumps to their bottoms. Girls sewing scales onto their skin, tentacles into their torsos. Girls inserting too-large, glowing eggs up inside themselves, the eggs shining through their stomachs. Girls with scissors in hand, hacking off the plump of their stomachs. Girls hacking off limbs. Girls tearing off their skin, stepping out of their bodies, and decorating their skeletons with pearls. Girls doing endless things Niamh had never even imagined.

'Christ,' Niamh whispered.

Aoife smirked, then shrugged. '"Beauty" is a big word. Who knows what he's into?'

Niamh opened her mouth to reply, but a door slammed open. They both turned towards the noise. In the doorway, the feathered doctor and the floating fairy king.

Full, cupid's-bow lips. Blue eyes, big smile, white teeth. Muscled and broad, tall, with tanned limbs that looked strong and sturdy in tight-fitting clothing. He was beautiful. He looked like a model Niamh couldn't remember the name of and a superhero on a big screen and every father she had ever wanted to be held by. His face was generic and forgettable in its perfection.

He leaned down to whisper something to the doctor. She smiled and began to address the room.

'Beauty contest is cancelled. The king has read your papers and made his decision,' she said. She raised a talon and pointed it at Niamh. Niamh's heart jerked upwards, elated.

'You.'

'Me?' Niamh asked. The doctor laughed.

'Nope, sorry, pointing at your friend.'

Behind her, Niamh heard giggles from the other girls. Blood rushed to her face as her heart fell back down.

'But I don't want to go,' Aoife said. She shook her head rapidly, backing away. She stumbled into the vanity, knocking over the bottles of makeup. Murmurs around the room.

'Why? What's wrong with you?' the doctor asked, talons growing longer. Every single person in the room was staring at them, whispering. Niamh could see Aoife looking at her for backup, eyes wide and panicked.

'Niamh?' she whispered, and touched her elbow. Her friend was looking at her for help.

Niamh looked down at her feet.

'Enough.'

The king had spoken, voice light and rich as whipped cream. He clicked his fingers. The warmth of Aoife's body next to her suddenly vanished; Niamh whipped her head back. Aoife was gone. So were the fairy king and feathered doctor.

No, Niamh thought. *No, no.*

The room was abuzz with noise, complaints, confusion, as she sat there, staring at the place where Aoife had been.

'Do we just go?' a girl across from her asked.

Slowly, the girls began to shuffle through the door out of the hall. Niamh stood, looking around her uncertainly. She followed the crowd out through the door because she didn't know what else to do.

*

The sun was too bright when Niamh emerged. She squinted as she stared back, trying to make herself leave.

The castle was surrounded by dragons and electric fencing. The dragons flew above in slow, lazy circles. Her stomach churned at their enormity but she knew they couldn't see her. Most were too old, and almost entirely blind. Fungus grew over their bodies, scales peeling like old wallpaper.

When Niamh was small, her mam bought her a Barbie Dreamtopia castle. It was a neon-pink glory. It dripped glitter and shine, floral sparkled décor plastered up the sides. There were butterflied doors and rainbowed towers and every inch of it stank of plastic and chemicals. This castle looked and smelled almost exactly like that, except it was unnervingly large and horrifically real. The gleaming doll plastic was terrifying on this scale—she couldn't even see where the towers ended, rising into the sky and out of sight. The leviathan size of it made her feel like she might just scream.

She forced herself to look away. She kept close to the shadows on her walk home, avoiding the sun. Her mam opened the door to their house before Niamh could even knock.

'How'd it go?' she asked. 'Was it Joan Hardy? Or Betty from down the road, lovely figure on her. Oh! Or little Sinead, she's just such a good girl, isn't she? So quiet. Or—'

'Aoife.'

'What?'

'He picked Aoife.'

Her mam blinked at her. Her mouth twisted, a thin knot of confusion.

'Aoife?'

'Yeah,' Niamh said, and pushed past her mam into the house. Her mam followed.

'But I thought she didn't want to do the test. You told me she was dreading it.'

'She obviously still had to do it,' Niamh said, trying to undo the buttons on her coat. Her fingers fumbled, fat and useless.

'No need for cheek. I meant, did she not refuse? Did she say no?'

'No. I mean, I don't know. Sort of.'

'"Sort of"? What do you mean, "sort of"?'

'Yeah, she did. She said she didn't want to go.'

'And what, she went anyway? What about you, what did you do?'

Niamh couldn't undo the last button. She pulled it back and forth, yanking at it. She growled, frustrated, and ripped the coat open. The button popped off, falling to the tiles of the floor with a clattering noise. Both Niamh and her mam stared at it.

'Niamh,' her mam said in a hushed voice, stepping closer to her. 'What happened?'

Niamh felt her mam's hand on her arm. She jerked away, recoiling. 'Don't touch me,' she said. Mam moved towards her again, and Niamh stepped away, scrambling backwards up the stairs.

She locked the door to her room and sank down against it. She looked at the spot on her that Mam had touched. She longed for a steel scrubber, a scrap of sandpaper, a hard-bristled brush.

She leaned her head against the frame. On the other side of the door, her mam murmured something that sounded like scolding and apologising all at once.

❧

Niamh stared up into the darkness of the ceiling.

She couldn't sleep—it was too quiet. No intrusions. Only her thoughts.

She wanted intrusion. She wanted distraction.

She wanted the bang of fireworks. She wanted the boom of a bomb killing thousands. She wanted a marching band and an angry mob and a nuclear explosion. She wanted the clatter of her mam bursting through the door to bang pots and pans. Wanted the sloppy slap of metal on meat as her mam beat her to death with them.

Instead, the scratch of her hands digging into the quilt, the muted growl of a car driving far away. Stifled movements rising from the rooms below. Insubstantial as spectre; Mam's inaudible heartbeat, the thought of her sighs.

Her ears pricked at a rustling outside. She looked towards the window, but the curtains were drawn. She stood up and went to open them, the wood of the floor cool under her feet. As she pulled the pale cotton to the side, the sound grew louder, urgent.

The garden outside was murky in semi-moonlight, a formless gloom. In the corner of the window, a piece of paper rattled against the glass, rustling quicker and quicker. She opened the window and reached out, grabbing the sheet. She pulled her hand back in but leaned forward, wanting to feel the breeze on her face.

The night air was warm, utterly still.

She looked down at the sheet, holding it close to the window to see more clearly. The light was poor, but the sheet seemed to be mostly blank. Towards the top of the page, there was a scribble of writing; she held the paper closer, squinting. *Aoife Delaney* was written in a scratched scrawl in a corner on the left side of the sheet. The letters flopped vicariously to the left, so tilted that they looked like they might stumble and fall from the page.

She scrunched the page in her hand, squashing it into a spiked ball. She gripped it tight, then dropped it; it felt hot to the touch, burning her fingers. The ball fell soundlessly to the floor. It lay there for a moment, then rose, the paper unfurling like a flower in bloom.

The sheet hovered in front of her, level with her face. It began to move, sliding around itself, the wrinkles rippling in contortions as it shifted in the air. It coiled its form, morphing jaggedly, before smoothing out into a hollow oval with two cupid-bowed points. It had formed itself into a smiling mouth.

The mouth opened. 'She is being raped,' it said, its sides up-turned. Its voice was raspy, a little high-pitched. It sounded like Aoife.

'She is smart, so she has already tried to piss herself because she knows that it can deter men. She is screaming "fire," because she knows people are more likely to help stop a fire than to help stop a rape. But no one is coming. She is struggling and bucking and her wrists are being held down and—'

Niamh grabbed at the paper. It swooped out of her grip, flitting behind her.

'She is having a bubble bath,' it continued. 'Steam rises from the bath, bringing with it the scent of lavender, vanilla, eucalyptus oil. Petals float on the surface of the water. The fairy king is floating over the bath, feeding her grapes. He holds out a flute of champagne. "For my queen," he says. "Thank you, my king," she simpers, eyelashes batting—'

'Aoife wouldn't simper,' Niamh said, jumping to grab it. The page flew higher, then dove down, circling her feet.

'She is being sold. The king is putting her on a boat, and she is going somewhere far away. Her arms are bound behind her back and she is being shoved into the hands of greasy-eyed strangers and they are touching her and money is being handed over and the king is walking away and—'

Niamh kicked at it, then dove down to catch it, bashing her knees against the wooden floor. She hissed, pain pulsing through the spot. The paper slowed, a corner of the sheet kissing her elbow as it breezed around her.

'She is cooking a roast dinner. She is wearing an apron. Her lips are painted red, and her hair is perfectly coiffed. Robins fly above her head, landing on her shoulders, and deer peek their heads through the window. One of the deer reaches through the window and smacks her ass with a hoof. She giggles and blushes. "Honey, I'm home," the fairy king calls from another room, and Aoife trips over her own kitten heels in her desperation to get to him—'

The page let out a breathy giggle midsentence, its smile widening as Niamh struggled to get up, holding her knee.

'Really,' the page said, its voice warm, 'she is being chopped up. Her body lies in pieces on a medical table, the fairy king standing above her in scrubs and a surgical mask. Bits of her remain recognisable—the freckles on her left arm, the brown strands of her hair. But mostly she is meat. The king raises a butcher knife high above his head, and brings it sharply down, and it goes into the neck and the splattering noise is—'

Niamh smacked the page from the air, slapping it into her desk. It crumpled flat against the surface, like a sad, squashed spider. It twitched a little and then was still. Niamh stepped back. She rubbed her eyes, her head and knee aching.

The page flew up into the air, shooting to the ceiling.

'She is lighting candles.' The page's voice was louder. It sharpened its consonants, like Aoife did when she was worked up. 'She is wearing a long, flowing white gown, and she is trembling. The king comes up behind her, putting his arms around her. "Don't worry, I'll be gentle," he says. She smiles gratefully. "I'm just so nervous, it's my first time," she murmurs back. He kisses her bare feet, her shaking hands.'

The page dove towards her, skimming her hair. It landed on her shoulder, then leapt to the other.

'He is not gentle,' it whispered, tickling her earlobe. 'She is so scared. She's screaming for you. And you're not there.'

Niamh stepped back. The paper followed, chasing her movements. She sat down on the bed, resting her head in her hands. The page fluttered around her, brushing its corners against her cheek, the tip of her nose.

Slowly, Niamh reached up and stroked its side, running a finger along its thin length.

The page shuddered. It retreated, falling backwards and tumbling through the air. It cartwheeled in circles, turning faster and faster, until it looked like hundreds of pages spinning all at once.

The spinning stopped, and hundreds of pages flew outwards.

Niamh looked up at them, dazed. They surrounded her on all sides, a flurry of sheets swirling like snow. They flew in a circle, gathering her in among them. They pulled closer and closer, clumping together, twisting and scrunching their bodies in union.

The flurry slowed, the pages solidifying in union as a shape tried to take form. The shape converged together, and Niamh found herself held.

Two paper arms enveloped her, wrapping around her waist. A paper neck leaned over her shoulder, a paper cheek pressed to her own. A flimsy forehead, nuzzling into her, the touch so frail, so light, that it could have been the brush of an insect's wing.

There was no voice. Niamh was silent, and so were the pages. The paper body had no mouth.

Niamh tried to remain still. The pages felt delicate around her. A puff of wind could send them tumbling. She held her breath, held her arms in place at her sides, held in the sound that was building and building in her skull and in her stomach and rising in waves up and up through her throat. She held it there, feeling the weight of that awful, unspeakable thing on her tongue.

She held herself in place. If she moved, it might all fall apart.

THE VEGETABLE

Mairead picked up the mug, inspecting it. She ran a finger along its rim, slowing down and pausing at the faint hairline fracture running along its side. 'You shouldn't use the dishwasher,' she said. She set the mug down on the kitchen table.

Bridget cupped her mug tight. The heat stung her hands, but she concentrated on keeping her expression neutral. 'I don't.'

'By hand, you know. Better, that. Your mam would have.' Her aunt dipped her finger into the coffee, swirling it. She popped her finger in her mouth, sucked lightly, then grimaced. The lines around her mouth deepened as her lips puckered. 'Your milk is spoiled.'

Bridget picked up her own, taking a sip. She could feel lumps of curdled milk against her lips. She took a long, deep swallow, then another, gulping it down until the cup was empty. She set it down and looked at her aunt. 'Yum,' she said, and licked her teeth, her tongue swollen and scalded.

Mairead shook her head. She picked up the two mugs and brought them to the sink, pouring her coffee down the drain. She began washing them by hand.

Bridget watched her aunt's back, the fat, sunburnt hump at the top of her spine. It twitched as her aunt worked, sensitive to movement. Bridget had the same lump on her own back. 'There's a man, in the field over,' Mairead said. 'In a camper van.'

'Oh?'

Mairead glanced back at her, examining her face. Bridget tried to make her mouth go round with surprise. 'Oh!' she repeated, raising her eyebrows up and down like she had seen people do on the TV.

'You should lock your doors.' Mairead gestured towards the front of the house with one of the mugs, sending a spray of water through the air. 'Anything could happen. On your own.'

'I do.' She didn't. She kept the doors unlocked at night and often left them wide open so she could lie in front of them and listen to the groans of the field as she fell asleep.

'But don't be rude to him. He's renting the space from the neighbours down the road.' Mairead dried the mugs with a dishcloth, rubbing them until they squeaked. She set them down and turned back to Bridget, putting her hand on her hips. 'Don't go thinking you're something special,' she said.

Bridget smiled widely, showing her gums. 'Ha!' she said. She enunciated the *h* sound heavily, to emphasise the humour. She slapped the table, then slapped her knee for good measure. 'Ha ha ha!'

Mairead looked down at her, brow furrowed. She rubbed her face, her eyes. Her hand was wet from the washing and left a trail of suds on her cheek. She grabbed her coat from the back of the chair. 'I'm off. I'll be back for the veg.' She put the coat on, looking out the window. Her face warmed, the lines melting into her skin like butter under sun. 'That's a beautiful harvest.'

Bridget stopped smiling. She looked out the window, at the rows of tall, red stalks. 'Yes. It is, isn't it?'

Mairead leaned down towards her. Bridget felt her aunt's lips on her scalp, the bone-hard press of her mouth. Bridget blinked into her neck. Her aunt's throat was a deep tan and smelled of stale tobacco, muted with a thick, smooth layer of Sudocrem.

'There's a good girl,' Mairead murmured, wrapping the words around the strands of Bridget's hair.

Her aunt closed the door as she left. Bridget opened it again the moment she heard the car drive away. She lay down on the floor parallel and crossed her arms across her chest, tucking them tightly into her sides. She closed her eyes.

She thought about the man her aunt mentioned. What would she do, she wondered, if he slunk through her door, or crept up to the window? She had seen a video of an ape pulling apart a small, furred animal before. It didn't need a weapon, or even its teeth; it was the wet, shameful sound of tearing she remembered now.

Perhaps he wouldn't physically assault her, but would stare in the window, lower his hand to his genitals, slowly stroke himself. If she screamed or turned away, would her disgust encourage him? Would ignoring him encourage him? Would staying still, her eyes shut tight, simply push his excitement higher?

She giggled, sighed, feeling her heart unwind.

'Hi,' a voice said.

Bridget opened her eyes. A man stood in the doorway, looking down at her. He was blocking the sun.

Bridget tried to rise quickly, stumbling slightly. 'Sorry,' she said.

She dusted her legs with her hands, then stopped when the man looked at the dirt on her knees.

The man leaned against the doorway, one leg crossed over the other. He was tall, head grazing the top of the frame. His large, luxurious mouth smiled down at her. 'I think we're neighbours,' he said. He sounded vaguely American. He pointed out the door with a thumb. 'I'm staying in the camper van across the way.'

She could feel the tendons of her neck tightening. Her nails bit into her palm. She nodded, tried to unclench. She held out her hand. 'Bridget.'

The man looked at the hand. He lowered his eyes to her ankles, then her stomach, then her clavicles. His gaze stung, leaving those spots raw and warm as a paper cut. Bridget dropped her hand.

'Are you scared?' he asked. His eyes flicked back up to her.

'What?'

'You seem nervous. Are you afraid of me?'

'I don't know what you mean.'

The man stepped forward. The motion brought him over the threshold of the door, into her home. The furniture looked smaller, older, with him inside the room.

'Are you all alone here?' He looked around, licked his lips.

Bridget's legs were loose and hot, like candle wax melting away from her body. 'What was your name?' she asked.

The man laughed. He stepped back out on the porch, no longer blocking the sun. Light spilled past the side of his head, blurring his expression to shadow. 'Just wanted to stop by. I'll leave you alone.'

He tapped the door with his knuckles. The knock was harder than she expected, the sound echoing loudly in the empty house.

✣

She waited until the evening to pick the harvest.

The bugs were giddy under the darkening sky. Beetles and ear-wigs swarmed the pathway while furred, rippling centipedes fell over one another to writhe in the cool, purpling light. A cluster of midges followed the heat of her skin as she walked down to the field, thick as fog around her face. She paid them no mind, easily sucking them up into her nostrils with each breath. Their wiry bodies stuck in her throat as she swallowed them down. She ran her tongue along her upper palate to catch a lingering of wings.

The sheep were calmer than the bugs. Morning time filled them with great distress, Bridget had noticed. The spilling of light, heat, colour, drove them to panic. The rise of a new day brought nothing but scrambling legs, screams.

But now, in the evening, they sank back on their stems, easing peacefully into their vegetation. Bridget tiptoed through the field as she passed, trying to keep quiet. Some had already sloped off into sleep, eyes closed. Others were conscious but did not appear present, gaze distant under relaxed brows. Their floating was beatific, smiles blissful as saints as they hung limply from their stalks.

When Mam was still here, she was the one who picked the sheep. She would walk through the pathway ahead of Bridget, her eyes at half-mast. She'd hold her palm up, moving it in slow circles. She'd pause from time to time, rolling her neck from side to side. Suddenly, she'd grab one of the sheep and hold their head to her own. She'd press her nose to the sheep's hair, sniffing loudly while grabbing the meat of its underbelly in a vise grip. Sometimes she'd lick the sheep's face, prodding the stained fur around its eyes with the tip of her tongue.

This one, Mam would say. Bridget would ask why, and Mam would shrug, or roll her eyes, or tell her to run ahead. One time, she was quiet for a moment. Then she said *it wants it the most*.

Bridget walked through the field, holding her right palm up. She felt the movement of wind on the skin, the slight heaviness of moisture in the air, and nothing more. She dropped her palm.

The sheep that registered her presence wept, bucking against the plants as she passed. Some rolled their bodies and batted their lids, beseeching with wet lashes. They threw themselves outwards, tugging on their stem and trying to launch themselves towards the knife in Bridget's left hand.

She slowed when she reached the rot-sheep. It was quiet as it looked at her, its eyes alert. It looked down at the tool. It lifted its head and smiled at Bridget, a slow, toothy grin. Its teeth were square and blunt, the same size as her own.

Bridget reached over, stroked its cheek. She saw its infected roots had grown darker in colour, glossy maroon. They leaked an orange pus that smelled of pickled onions. *Bad fruit*, she thought. It would be unusable. 'I'm sorry,' she said, and moved away.

The rot-sheep began to scream immediately, thrashing violently. Bridget ignored it and walked on. She held her palm up again, trying to know what her mother had known. She walked in circles and knew nothing. When her feet grew sore, she stopped. She turned to the sheep she had stopped next to and held up the knife. 'Congrats,' she said.

The sheep beamed, squealing and wobbling its head in a little dance. Bridget placed the knife against the stem of the plant, lodged into the centre of the sheep's spine. She began to saw. The stem spurted forcefully, the red sap splattering over her hands. It was hot and oily to touch, like burnt grease poured from a pan.

The sheep moaned as she cut, the sound breathy and sweet in the summer air.

⊰⊱

The sap stained her hands. She was able to wash most of it off under hot water, but the temperature had to be so high that it scalded her hands and left the skin peeling. The sap also dried under the nails and was harder to remove. She used her teeth to get it out, biting the nails to the quick and scraping the skin with her incisors to remove the dark crust. She expected it to taste salty, like blood, but it was closer to sweetened wild garlic, aromatic and pungent with a subtle honey note that tickled the back of her throat.

Bridget left the work shed when she was done with the sheep, rubbing her hands against her trousers. The sap had been harder to get off than usual, the remaining thin layer gluing her fingers together in scarlet webbing.

Bridget looked down at her hands. The red was bright, a healthy shade indicative of the quality of the fruit. The dark mould of the rot-sheep was a devastation, in comparison. An evil thing, she thought, to wait and wait forever, for nothing.

Suddenly, her skin felt too tight, her stomach turning. She began to walk, taking deep breaths to try to calm herself. She avoided the harvest, skirting the edges of the field and around, until she was at the border between her field and the next.

It had grown darker while she had worked on the sheep, but she could still make out the camper van at the other side of the field. The fence between the fields was low, a weather-worn wooden barrier that reached just over her thighs. She hiked one leg up and over it, and then the other.

As she marched towards it, the camper van became clearer. It looked old, rust crusting the corners of the metal. Up close, she saw that there were flags stuck along its side: USA, Italy, Korea, Sweden, Brazil, and more, some she couldn't place. She approached the door and stood there. She could hear muffled television sounds through it, a muted laugh track. She knocked hard, bashing her fist against the frame. A moment later, the door opened.

The man looked down at her. His full mouth thinned in a line, creeping into a snarl. He held a hammer in his hand, half-raised.

'Hello,' Bridget said, looking at the hammer.

The man lowered the hammer but didn't drop it completely. 'Hello.'

Bridget looked past him, trying to see inside the caravan, but the room was dark. The glow of a television threw some light on a foldable chair, larger cans, a box of tissues, but she could see little else.

'I'm not frightened of you,' she said, looking back to him.

His mouth relaxed. His hand twitched around the handle of the hammer. 'Is that right?'

She nodded. The man lifted the hammer. He drew it back, holding it like he would strike. He tapped the doorframe with the hammer, almost playful. He watched her face, measuring.

She took a step forward. He lowered the hammer and stepped back, leaning away from her.

'Do you want me to feel frightened?' she asked.

The sound of the television grew louder. She had thought she had heard a laugh track, but she now could hear it was just one man laughing, then groaning, grunting. Someone else sobbed, over and over; the sound reminded her of the sheep, which made her smile.

'What's your name?' she asked him, still smiling.

The man was not smiling. He glanced back behind him and shifted his body, blocking the inside of the camper van from her view. He tossed the hammer between his hands. 'John. My name is John.'

'It's nice to meet you, John.'

John's grip tightened on the hammer again, flexing briefly. She stepped back. Night had fallen fully, the fields swallowed whole by the dark.

'You should come visit,' she said. 'We're all alone.'

❧

She woke before the sheep. She stretched on the floor, soaking in the calm of the morning like a cool pool of water. It coated her as she moved through velvet air and out of the house, supple with silence.

John was already there, standing by the porch. He faced away from her, towards the field. His back wide, stretching the thin, white cotton of his T-shirt. She could see his skin through the transparent material, reddened with sunburn.

'That looks sore,' she said. He didn't turn around.

'I was somewhere hot.'

'Where?'

He stood up. 'I've never seen them before, in person.'

She stood beside him. Sharp streaks of sunrise split the field, slicing into the harvest. The light was waking the sheep. They mewled at first, sluggish and tired, then shrieked as they became alert.

'We're lucky to have them,' she said.

She picked up the watering hose from beside the door and walked down to the field. She took the sheep one by one, dousing their roots and leaves.

She usually didn't bother with watering, the sheep-plant being resilient as it was, but the summer had been dry. The crumbling earth melted instantly as the cold water hit it, giving in to the moisture with sludging relief. The sheep halted their cries for a moment as they were watered, blinking in shock at the sensation.

John followed beside her, watching her work. He didn't talk, observing wordlessly. She stopped when they reached the rot-sheep. The mould had begun to spread into the leaves, pustulous purple veins running like ore through the foliage. She lifted the hose and then lowered it again, unsure whether to water it or not.

John halted beside her, in sync with her movements. He looked at her, head tilted.

'It's sick,' Bridget said.

'Oh.' John had been raising a hand towards the sheep. He dropped it. 'Is it infectious?'

'No. Not to us or the other sheep. It's just no good to us.'

Bridget lifted the hose over the roots and then doused the leaves. The sheep hummed, the sound almost a purr. It leaned towards her, nuzzling its face against Bridget's shoulder.

'What's the point in watering it?' John asked.

Bridget shrugged.

They walked on. The rich smell of damp earth rose as they moved through the field, almost metallic. By the time Bridget had watered each plant, the ground was fudgy and moist as chocolate cake under foot, the squidging slop of it oozing between the toes of her sandals. They emerged on the other side of the harvest, the camper van in the distance.

'I have to do the rest on my own,' Bridget said. 'I have to pick one to harvest.'

John held out his T-shirt, flicking at mud stains. The movement revealed a sliver of his stomach. It was pale, slightly rounded. 'How do you pick them?' he asked, scraping his nails on the cotton.

'It's hard. They all want it.'

John dropped the T-shirt. 'They want it?'

She nodded.

'Does it feel good?' he asked.

Bridget pressed her feet down into the mud, wanting to sink deep into it. 'I don't think it feels good in the way that you mean,' she said.

John frowned. 'What do you mean, then?'

'You have to understand what it's like, for them. Change, any kind of change. It would feel ecstatic, even if it was a bad thing. Even bad change. Do you understand?'

John smiled. He looked over her body and took a step closer. He leaned down, pressing his mouth near her ear. 'Can I watch?' he asked, the words warm on the lobe.

A wave of coldness rushed through Bridget, like all her blood had poured out through her feet. She felt nauseated, stomach swooping.

'No,' she said. 'It's private.'

She walked back into the field to do her work. She didn't look back.

❧

She chose a sheep at random. She didn't bother raising her palms to sense vibrations in the air. She looked around for a moment when she reached the centre of the field and then picked the first one that caught her eye.

She got the knife from the house, then came back to cut it down, walking to the shed with it under her arm. It wiggled about as it tried to look around, squirming in her grip. It squealed when they emerged from the harvest, head spinning on its neck to take in the startling new sights.

She balanced the sheep on her hip while opening the shed door, tucking it into the crook between hip and waist. Inside, the unlit room was dusty, the shadows pillowy as clouds.

She flicked on the light and placed the sheep on the preparation table. It lay on its back and beamed up at her, kicking its legs like an overexcited baby.

She took out the tools from below the table. She raised each one up for the sheep to look at, letting it sniff and lick the tool for inspection before she placed it on the table beside it. When she took out the radio, the sheep snorted, nosing it firmly.

'Of course,' Bridget said, and switched it on, searching through the stations. The sheep tilted its head and listened. It nodded firmly when she reached a station playing opera. The sound of bellowing harmonies filled the room, hazy with static.

She started the harvest with a bubble bath. She set the sheep in the soapy tub, plopping in a sparkling bath bomb so that the sheep could watch it fizz. The bomb left a layer of glitter on the surface of the water. Bridget reached in and gathered a palmful. She rubbed it through the sheep's curls, massaging it deep into the roots. She repeated the process with a palmful of olive oil, rosemary serum, lavender cream. The curls grew silken and lush, glistening with health.

She held up a mirror for the sheep to see. It gasped, then smiled. It made a sound that resembled a throaty laugh.

She lifted the sheep from the bath, its wet, perfumed body soaking her clothes. She took out a fluffy towel and a wide-toothed comb, brushing and drying the curls with care. The sheep closed its eyes while she worked, humming along with the music.

When the fur was dry, she grabbed the shaver from the table. She held it out for the sheep to see. 'Okay?' she asked. The sheep nodded.

She shaved the sheep quickly. The freshened curls fell in piles on the floor. The naked sheep swayed from side to side, testing the air on its bare skin. It seemed pleased, wiggling its bottom in time with the radio. It walked over to the table, lifting itself up. It looked over at Bridget, bleated questioningly.

'We could do some other stuff, first, if you would like?' Bridget said. 'I have an aromatherapy set, body oils for a massage. I've even got a kit for pedicures. Nice, to relax, if you wanted.'

The sheep bleated again, firmly. Bridget returned to the table and picked up a knife. 'Okay, lie back.'

The sheep stretched out. Bridget put her hand on its round tummy. She leaned down, kissed its belly button lightly. She blew into its chub, making a farting noise. The sheep wheezed, a whining, guttural giggle.

Bridget straightened up. She placed the knife at the start of its neck, pointing the tip of the blade just below its throat.

She pushed down. It sliced through easily, like cutting into a bowl of jelly. She cut from its collarbones down to crotch, the line clean and straight. The sheep sighed, the sound fluttering and pleased.

She held the line of the incision open with her hands. She reached inside the gash, moving her fingers through the tender folds with care. Under her fingertips, she felt the sheep throb.

She picked up the insides as gently as she could. They were slippery and wet, sliding through her fingers in a way that made Bridget hollow with fear. The delicate weight of them reminded her of fragile teacups, baby birds, things to be cared for and not dropped. She pulled the organs out one by one, lowering them to the storage container on the floor.

She worked slowly. The sheep cooed and purred, its muscles relaxing into the table. Bridget paused her movements for a moment, and it snorted in annoyance, kicking Bridget's side until she continued.

She scooped out the sheep until it was empty. It raised its head and looked down at itself, peering into the gaping split. It raised its hoof, trailing it down the edge of the wound, and dipped inside. Bridget glanced away, feeling like an intruder.

The sheep removed its hoof and gestured to Bridget, calling her over. It tilted its neck back, exposing its throat.

'Yeah?'

The sheep nodded. She placed the tool against the sheep's throat.

She thought about saying something. *You were a good sheep. I love you. Take me with you. This part might hurt, but I hope it does not.* She said nothing and cut its throat in a single motion.

'Did you like that?'

She spun around, startled by the sudden voice. John stood at the door, watching. He rubbed his thighs with his hands.

'I said you couldn't be here.'

John smiled. 'I liked it. A lot.'

Bridget stepped in front of the sheep, wanting to block it from his line of sight. John came closer, craning his head to see.

The sound of a car pulling up outside made the two of them jump. John looked towards the noise, wincing. He looked back at the sheep briefly, grinning, and left. Bridget stood for a moment, unable to move. She listened to his footsteps as he walked off, then she listened to his absence.

She walked over to the bathtub and unplugged it. The curls and glitter swirled as the water drained, strands of hair knotting in a narrowing dance.

On the table, the heft of the bald, dead sheep splayed itself out, its life spread open wide.

⁂

Mairead's car was parked in the driveway. Bridget ran her hand along its side as she approached the house. The metal was still warm.

The front door was closed, though Bridget had left it open this morning. She knocked on the wood. Inside, the sound of a scraping chair, shuffling feet, then the movements ceased.

It felt like a minute passed, or two. Then another minute and another. She pressed her face against the wood, the dry splinters scraping her cheeks.

The door opened, and Bridget lifted her head, moving back. Mairead stood in front of her, her crossed arms filling the entrance. 'You're a fool.'

'Can I come in?'

'I saw him leaving the shed. Have you any sense?'

Bridget shrugged. Mairead shook her head and stepped aside. Bridget walked in, heading to the kitchen. She flicked on the kettle.

'Sit down,' Mairead said. She shouldered Bridget out of the way and reached over the sink to get the mugs.

Bridget sat down. 'I told him he wasn't allowed to go in there. I said no.'

'More fool you.'

Mairead made coffee and handed Bridget a mug. She opened the fridge and took out the milk, shaking it at Bridget. She opened it and held it upside down over the sink.

'There's something I need to talk to you about,' Mairead said. The milk moved down the bottle slowly, the spoiled cream solidified to jelly.

'The innards from the harvest are in the shed. Two this week.' Bridget took a sip of the coffee, black and unsweetened. It tasted like nothing; she missed the sour curds.

Mairead looked up at her. 'Two?'

'Two.'

'How long did you keep them alive?'

'Until the end of the harvesting.'

The milk made a squelching noise as its slopped out of the bottle in a chunky, curdled clump. 'That's good. That's very good. Better, you know.'

Mairead sat down. Her hands were empty of any mug, which made Bridget nervous.

'Tea?' Bridget asked, half rising.

'I'm going to die.'

Bridget sat back down.

'Not right now,' Mairead said. 'But one day you're going to be here, alone. You're going to look after the harvest, and do my selling, and you'll do it alone.' Mairead reached over and took Bridget's hand. Mairead's palm felt dry and rough as sandpaper. 'I need you to have more sense.'

'I'm good with the sheep.'

'It's not about being good at it. It's about being good at it forever. You're going to get older too. And you have no little ones.'

'I don't want little ones.'

'I know. You shouldn't. You're no mother. But it means there's no one to take over for you.'

Bridget tried to take her hand back, but Mairead gripped it tight, her blunt nail rammed into Bridget's skin. Bridget gripped back tighter. She squeezed her aunt's fingers hard enough that she could feel the fragility of the brittle bones beneath, like overcooked clay. Mairead didn't let go, but nodded, looking pleased.

'This is it,' Mairead said. 'And it's yours.'

After Mairead left to collect the harvest from the shed, Bridget paced the house.

She walked from room to room, placing her hands on the walls to feel that they were solid and not made of cardboard or papier-mâché. She stood in her mother's bedroom and picked up objects and held them close, inspecting them. An empty bottle of apricot body spray, a torn hand fan, a folder of clippings from *National Geographic*. A cactus husk, a box of condoms, a deflated balloon.

She recognised nothing.

She opened up the window in her mother's room, then the windows in her own room, the kitchen, the bathroom, the sitting room and the hall. She opened the back door wide, though the back was half-sunk in marsh water and the open door would attract the slimed, gnarled creatures that resided within.

She opened the front door and lay down in front of it. She closed her eyes and tried to hold her breath until she passed out, pinching her mouth and nose closed with her hands. Her mind was helium-light, rising away from her bones.

She opened her eyes and evening had taken hold. A pair of moths fluttered over her head, their wings tickling the tip of her nose. She brushed them away, looking out towards the field.

It wasn't bright enough to see the bugs on the ground, but she could hear them, the crack and squidge of their shells as her bare feet broke them open. She walked down into the harvest with the knife in her hand, the world tinged blue in the disappearing light.

The rot-sheep was still awake. The mould had risen up its body, molten patches of infected skin left balding and grey.

'Do you want to come with me?' Bridget asked. 'I don't think it'll save you.'

The sheep whined, throwing itself into Bridget's body. Bridget wrapped her arms around the sheep, nuzzling into its foul, fluffy neck. 'Okay,' she said.

She placed the tool against its rotting stem and sawed through. The sheep shuddered in her arms as the stem spewed its pus, the thick, sticky substance coating Bridget's hands.

She lifted her hands to the sheep, running them through its dusty curls. The pus tangled in the hair, saturated streaks of luminous rot.

She took the sheep's head in her hands to look at it. The strange, square pupils and familiar eyes, a cutting, knowing gaze. She kissed the furry eyebrows and wiry cheeks, its small, shining nose.

She carried the sheep on her shoulder as she returned to the house, patting its back and bottom to make it coo and chirp. It weighed very little; she assumed most of its insides had rotted by now, sinking out into the stem.

She brought it to her bedroom. When she opened the door, she paused. John stood in the centre of the room, looking down at her bed.

She put the sheep down gently. She took a step forward, her shoes loud on the wood, but John didn't seem to notice. His breathing was heavy and loud in the quiet. She approached him and touched his shoulder. He jerked under her hand, spinning around.

His eyes were wide, alarmed, darting around wildly. He held his hands up, like a boxer cornered in a ring.

In one of his hands, he clutched a knife so tightly that it shook. In the other, he gripped a fistful of cable ties. One dropped on the ground; it looked like his hands were slippery with sweat. A medicinal bottle poked out of his pocket.

They looked at each other, John pale and shivering.

'Bridget,' he said.

Bridget approached again, holding her hands up in the air. 'Hi, John,' she said, waving one hand slowly. 'Are you okay?'

He stumbled away, shoving the knife in the other pocket.

'Hey, hey, careful.' Bridget hunched down slightly, trying to appear smaller. She smiled up at him. 'Only me, all alone,' she said.

John frowned. He took the knife back out of his pocket, holding it up; it looked like he wasn't sure whether to brandish the knife, or hand it over to her.

Bridget reached over and petted his hand, stroking it gently like a frightened bird. 'It's okay,' she said. 'You're okay.'

She placed her hand higher, touching his biceps. John's arm shook in her grip, a cold sheen of sweat covering the skin. She lifted the arm up, raising his hand to her neck. She guided the knife to her throat, feeling his wrist tremble against her clavicle.

She licked her lips, pressing her neck into it. 'Go on,' she said.

John dropped the knife.

He shoved past her, his pockets spilling everywhere in his haste to move. She followed him, but he was quick, darting out of the room and out the back door. She watched him slosh away through the marshes, the panicky jerks of his limbs, the half sobs of his frightened breath.

Chickenshit, she thought.

Bridget returned to the room. On the ground were the cable ties, the glass bottle, coins, a gag, and a set of keys. Car keys, she thought, maybe. Maybe a camper van, even.

She picked them up and slipped them into her trouser pockets. She jiggled them with her hand.

The sheep whined, squirming at the door. It was trying to come to her, but its legs were weak with rot and dragged along the ground. It clawed itself towards her, pushing its torso forward in small, violent jerks.

She went over and picked it up, holding it in her arms. She rocked it back and forth and swirled them around, twirling in a loose, lazy waltz. The sheep wobbled its head back and forth, moving in time with her steps. Rot leaked from its back, dripping over the two of them as they swayed together in the empty house.

They danced out of the bedroom, out of the open front door. Out onto the porch and out to the grass. The keys jinglejangled in her pockets, the sound light and sweet as clinking champagne flutes. They danced outwards, Bridget growing dizzy and giddy as they spun into the night.

The harvest spread out before them in welcome and the dark fields after that, a long stretch of ballroom brimming with life.

ACKNOWLEDGEMENTS

I would like to express my gratitude to the many individuals and organisations whose support has been instrumental in the completion of this collection.

I would like to thank my agent, Ed Wilson, for championing this book, as well as Anna Dawson and the entire Johnson and Alcock team. I am also deeply appreciative of my editors, Olivia Taylor Smith and Leah Woodburn, for their invaluable guidance, as well as their assistants, Brittany Adames, Rali Chorbadzhiyska and Brodie McKenzie. Special thanks to Tim O'Connell and Francis Bickmore for their support, as well as the rest of the teams at Simon & Schuster and Canongate.

I am grateful to the faculty and visiting writers at University College Cork, including Mary Morrissey, Thomas Morris, Danny Denton, and Sara Maitland, for their care and encouragement during a very formative time. I also extend my heartfelt thanks to the University of East Anglia faculty members Philip Langeskov and Naomi Woods, as well as writer and potter Andrew Cowan, for their advice and kindness during my creative writing studies.

I am appreciative of the feedback I have received from my

generous peers during the writing of this collection and thankful to my UEA creative writing cohort for their assistance in our workshops. In particular, I would like to thank Olivia Lowden, Ariane Parry and Gabrielle Griot for all their help during that year, and in the years since; I am fortunate to have these thoughtful, brilliant people in my life.

The financial support provided by the Quercus Programme Scholarship, Eoin Murray Memorial Scholarship, Malcolm Bradbury Memorial Scholarship, Ted and Mary O'Regan Bursary and the Arts Council of Ireland's Agility Award has been crucial in enabling me to dedicate time to my writing. I am grateful for these opportunities.

Growing up in Waterford, I was lucky to be surrounded by youth groups that encourage young artists and creatives. Thank you to Waterford Youth Arts and Ollie Breslin for providing a place for young people to find a love for art, and a place for me to write terrible poetry.

Thank you to my mam and my brothers—I love you very much. Thank you to Christopher for being my friend.

ABOUT THE AUTHOR

Rose Keating is a writer from Waterford, Ireland. She studied on the Creative Writing Prose Fiction MA at UEA, where she was a recipient of the Malcolm Bradbury Scholarship and the Curtis Brown Prize. She is a winner of the Marian Keyes Young Writer Award, the Hot Press Write Here, Write Now prize, and the Ted and Mary O'Regan Arts Bursary. She has been published in *The Stinging Fly*, *Apex Magazine*, *Banshee* and *Southword*. In 2022, she received an Agility Award from the Irish Arts Council to fund the completion of her debut short story collection.